The Woman
in the Bazaar

The Woman in the Bazaar

Alice Perrin

MINT EDITIONS

The Woman in the Bazaar was first published in 1914.

This edition published by Mint Editions 2021.

ISBN 9781513269610 | E-ISBN 9781513274614

Published by Mint Editions®

 MINT
EDITIONS

minteditionbooks.com

Publishing Director: Jennifer Newens
Design & Production: Rachel Lopez Metzger
Typesetting: Westchester Publishing Services

Contents

Chapter 1

The Vicar's Daughter

Summer-time at Under-edge compensated, in a measure, for the trials and severities of winter—for winter could be grim and cruel in the isolated little Cotswold village approached by roads that were almost perpendicular. Why such a spot should ever have been fixed upon for human habitation seemed difficult to comprehend, save that in old and dangerous days its very inaccessibility may have been its chief attraction; most of the villagers were descendants of gypsies, outlaws, and highwaymen. Now, at the close of the nineteenth century, no one, unless held by custom and tradition, or by lack of means, remained permanently at Under-edge; for communication with the world in the valley below was still conducted by carrier, postal arrangements were awkward and uncertain, water very often scarce, and existence during winter-time a long-drawn period of bleak and hard monotony.

But when the vast fields, bounded by rough stone walls, grew green and luscious, and the oaks put forth new foliage the colour of a young pea-pod, and the elm trunks sprouted feathery sprays that likened the trees to gigantic Houdan fowls, life in Under-edge became at least endurable. Even the dilapidated vicarage looked charming, wistaria draping the old walls in mauve cascades, and white montana creeper heaped above the porch; roses and passion flower climbed and clung to broken trellis-work, and outside the dining-room window the magnolia tree, planted by a former vicar many years ago, filled the air with lemon scent from waxen cups. Though the garden was unkempt, the grass so seldom mown, and the path unweeded, hardy perennials brightened the neglected flower-beds, and lilac, syringa, laburnum, flourished in sweet luxuriance. It was a paradise for birds, whose trilling echoed clear from dawn to sunset in this safe retreat.

Rafella Forte, the vicar's daughter, came out of the house this summer morning in a blue cotton frock that matched her eyes, wearing no hat on her yellow head. A coarse market basket was slung on her arm, and she carried a light pronged fork, since her object was not to cut flowers for the drawing-room vases, as would seem natural for a young lady, but to dig potatoes for the midday meal. The potato patch was perhaps the most useful portion of the vicarage garden, and it meant real disaster if the crop was scanty, since the living of Under-edge, though not quite so miserable as some, was yet poor enough to render the garden produce of infinite value, in support of one joint a week, an occasional hen that had ceased laying, and sometimes a rabbit presented by a farmer.

Ella Forte was barely twenty-one, yet for years had she worked, and scraped, and saved, so that the little household—herself, her father, and a single-handed servant—might subsist in tolerable comfort; that there might be something still in hand for parish claims, for possible emergencies, for, at least, a passably respectable appearance. She gloried in her management, she knew no discontent, she was proud to fill the post surrendered by her mother, who lay beneath a shrinking mound in the churchyard just beyond the vicarage domain. She was complacently convinced of her father's dependence upon her, and of her influence in the village, where she had no rival, for the squire's house stood empty, closed, falling into disrepair, its owner dwelling out of England, crippled by a dwindling rent-roll and heavy charges on the property.

This morning she sang blithely as she crossed the lawn that more nearly resembled a hay-field—sang one of the hymns she had selected for to-morrow's service, to be led by herself to her own strenuous accompaniment on the aged harmonium and the raucous voices of the village congregation. The sun shone on her hair, that glinted golden, crinkling over her little head, gathered into a then unfashionable knob at the nape of her slim, white neck. And Captain Coventry, riding along the road, looked over the privet hedge and thought he had never beheld anything on this earth to compare with its glory. Why, the girl's hair was like "kincob," like the border of a nautch woman's veil, like the work on a rajah's robe!

Captain Coventry had just returned from India, and the glamour of the East was still upon him—the East that is so very different to look back upon when a man's whole service need not be spent in exile. Just now he was on short leave, and his regiment—an English line regiment—would be returning home in two years' time. India, to him, was yet a pleasant quarter of the globe that meant sport (his passion) well within his means, cheaper comfort, cheaper living, amusements that were welcome to his outdoor tastes, not to speak of soldiering experiences of the finest next to active service. He was on a visit to his widowed mother and his spinster sister, who lived in the little country town lying at the base of the hills that jutted out like monstrous knuckles over the Severn Valley; and feeling slightly bored, in need of exercise, of movement, he had hired a horse and was exploring Cotswold villages on morning rides.

So it came about that on this perfect summer day he had passed through Under-edge, and was arrested now by the vision of a girl with golden head and bright blue gown in the garden of a wayside vicarage.

Involuntarily he checked his mount, and from behind the hedge he watched the slim blue figure move across the grass and stand for a moment outlined against a door in an ivy-covered garden wall. She was singing as she wrestled with a rusty latch:

> *"Other refuge have I none;*
> *Hangs my helpless soul on Thee;*
> *Leave, ah! leave me not alone,*
> *Still support and comfort me."*

How he wished he could see her face; he felt he *must* see it! And when she had opened the door and vanished from his view, he rode on slowly, reluctantly, scheming how he might return with some specious reason that would enable him to speak with her.

George Coventry was not susceptible. Save for a youthful and hopeless love affair that left no lasting impress on his heart, his life had been exceptionally free from sexual distractions; he was more on his guard against women than actually indifferent to them. Without conceit, he was not wholly unaware that he found favour, generally, with females of his class, the very austereness of his nature provoked and attracted them; but illicit love repelled him, and, so far, since he had been in a position to support a wife, no girl or woman in particular had caught his fancy, though in the abstract he was not averse to the notion of marriage.

His ideal of womanhood was modelled on the type represented by his mother and his aunts and his spinster sister, ladies whose sole charm lay in their personal virtue, the keynote of whose lives was duty and devotion to the home. Coventry was an only son, and on the death of his father his mother's whole existence became centred on himself, while Miss Coventry sacrificed youth and pleasure and all outside interests in order that she might minister undividedly to her bereaved parent; and both women remained serenely unconscious of the waste of life and energy and happiness that the sacrifice entailed. The daughter refused a proposal from a worthy gentleman because, she said, she could not leave Mama; and her mother and her brother accepted this decision as only right and proper. The suitor failing to suggest that Mama should also become an inmate of his house, the matter went no further. Such immolation of female youth to age is common and unending, and in the majority of cases the victim lays down her natural rights on the altar of duty with but little conception of the magnitude of the offering, and receives small credit for her martyrdom.

There had been something chaste and exquisite about this maiden in the garden that had touched a tender chord in George Coventry's breast. He felt an inward certainty that the girl was gentle, simple, sweet—a little saint, with her aureole of hair, and her artless singing of the old familiar hymn. The impression lured him so irresistibly that he was several times on the point of turning his horse's head, but each excuse that presented itself struck him as too thin. He had lost his way—where to? He had been suddenly taken ill, felt faint; the very idea caused him to smile—he had never felt faint in his life and did not know how to enact the symptoms, and no one would for a moment believe him to be ill, judging by his appearance of hopelessly robust health! Perhaps a cigarette would stimulate his imagination; he put his hand in his pocket and encountered a knife given him only yesterday by his sister for his birthday—the kind of gift "for a man" above which certain feminine minds seem unable to rise when cigarette-cases, sleeve-links, tie-pins and pocket-books have been exhausted. The knife was a cumbersome plated article, comprising, in addition to blades of all sizes, a corkscrew, folding scissors, a button-hook, and an instrument intended for the extraction of stones from horses' hoofs. For once he blessed Nellie's limited notions of masculine needs, because her present suggested a plausible plea.

He dismounted and searched about the ground for a pebble that might suit his purpose. Anyone passing would have supposed that the big, bronzed young man scraping in the dust of the country road must have dropped some treasured possession.

Presently he passed his hand with practised touch down the horse's fetlock, and the animal raised its hoof in docile response. Coventry wedged a little stone between the hoof and the shoe, then turned in the direction of the vicarage, the bridle over his arm, the horse limping, ever so slightly, behind him.

At the wooden entrance gate he paused. The vicarage front door stood open, and across the rough gravel sweep he could see into the hall—see a stone-paved floor and an oak chest, with hats and coats hanging from hooks above it. A rose-scented peace enveloped the house and garden; he heard no sound save the high, clear calling of birds.

A sudden reluctance assailed him, kept him standing at the gate, his hand on the latch, his heart beating fast; a fateful feeling that if he disturbed this somnolent calm his whole life, his whole future, would be affected, whether for evil or for good. The horse nuzzled his shoulder gently, a yellow butterfly skimmed past. He thought of the girl's golden hair in the sunshine, and he swung open the gate.

Ivy hid the door-bell, but he found it and pulled boldly. The result was disconcerting; never had he known a house-bell create such a clamour; it clanged and re-echoed, and continued till he felt it must surely rouse not only the vicarage but the entire village. Long before its pealing ceased a door was opened within, and an elderly cleric, with a grey beard and a benevolent expression, appeared in the porch.

Coventry raised his hat, apologised for his intrusion, and explained.

"My horse," he said, "has got a stone in his hoof, and I'm a long way from home. Have you anything you could lend me to get it out?"

That was the beginning. The vicar was cordially sympathetic, and at once went in search of some instrument, returning with a pruning knife, a skewer, and a chisel.

"Perhaps one of these?" he said, and then stood by, remarking upon the weather and the prospects of the fruit crop and the hay, and the unusual heat, while with much apparent effort the stone was extracted and cast aside.

Then Coventry stood up and mopped his forehead.

"Yes, the heat is extraordinary, I suppose, for England, though of course it's nothing compared with India."

"Ah! So you have had some experience of the tropics?"

"I'm home on leave from my regiment in India."

The vicar was interested. "Then, no doubt," he said, "you can tell me what headway conversion to Christianity is making among the heathen? I once contemplated joining an Indian mission myself, but there were difficulties in the way—my dear wife's health, the birth of my little daughter, and so forth. But it is a subject that has always attracted me strongly."

Coventry strove to recollect if he had ever conversed with a missionary in India. "I believe," he uttered profoundly, "that it is a very intricate question."

"Quite so; and at such a distance it is difficult for stay-at-homes to understand the obstacles that our brave workers have to encounter and overcome. Idolatry, from all accounts, is a very formidable foe. My daughter is just now organising a little sale of work, to be held here next week, in aid of foreign missions; we like to feel that, humble parish as we are, we do our small share to help. But I must not keep you standing in the sun. Will you not take your horse round to the stables and let us offer you a rest and some refreshment before you go on your way?"

Coventry displayed becoming hesitation. He could not think of giving so much trouble, of taking up the vicar's valuable time, though he admitted that a short halt would not be altogether unwelcome in view of the distance he had come and the distance he had still to go. He permitted himself to be persuaded, and his host conducted him to the back of the house, to where a couple of empty stalls and a coach-house almost in ruins faced a weed-choked yard appropriated now by poultry and some pigs.

They re-entered the house by the kitchen, that had a red-brick floor, an open range, and black beams across the low ceiling; they traversed a long flagged passage, passed through a swing-door that must once have been covered with green baize, and thence across the hall to the vicar's study. It was a cool and restful room despite its shabby furniture and musty odour.

"I always half expect to see my predecessor sitting in my chair," the vicar told him whimsically. "He was here for nearly half a century. These old vicarages are steeped in memories. I have been here myself for over twenty years, and I still feel as if I was a kind of interloper! Everything is practically just the same as when I took the living over. We move very slowly in these benighted mountain villages."

Someone passed the open window.

"Rafella!" called the vicar.

Coventry held his breath. What a charming name! Next moment he was gazing at a girl's face framed in passion-flower and roses; and the face was even fairer and more angelic than he had imagined. Delicate, clear-cut features, eyes of heavenly blue, a skin so pink and white that it might almost have been painted, and the hair—the glorious golden hair!

Afterwards he could never very clearly recall what followed. He knew he was introduced to "Rafella" as she stood at the window, that she came in and apologised prettily for the mould that stained her little hands—she said with engaging simplicity that she had been digging potatoes. He knew he was regaled with lemonade and water biscuits,

ALICE PERRIN

and that she sat and smiled, and looked like a Madonna, while her father talked of missions and asked innumerable questions concerning India. Was the heat out there actually so severe? Was there constant danger from snakes and wild beasts? Was it true that the social life was demoralising to the European? And how about the question of drink, and the example set in that respect, and others, by the English? Also, was it a fact that the Oriental was possessed of strange faculties that could not be explained, and had Captain Coventry himself ever seen a man climb up a rope and vanish into space?

All of which Captain Coventry answered to the best of his capability, the whole while cogitating how he might contrive his next meeting with the vicar's daughter. At last a casual reference to the coming sale of work presented an excellent opportunity.

"I wonder if I might bring my mother and my sister to the show?" he asked with diffidence. "They take such a keen interest in things of that description." And he explained how easy it would be to manage if he chartered a conveyance for the afternoon.

Naturally the idea met with cordial encouragement, and led to further interchange of personal information. By the time Captain Coventry had begun to feel that he could, with decency, remain no longer, he was on most friendly terms with the Reverend Mr. Forte and Rafella, the clergyman's only child.

Chapter 2

In the Garden

Until the day of the sale of work at Under-edge Vicarage Coventry lived through the hours as one in a dream, dominated by the mental vision of a gentle girl, by his ardent longing for the moment when he should see her face again. He realised that he had actually fallen in love at first sight, admitted the fact to himself with grudging reluctance, seeing that hitherto he had scoffed at belief in such a possibility—like a person who suddenly sees a ghost after contemptuous denial of the supernatural.

He intended to make the girl his wife. She might not be accomplished or clever; her education must necessarily have been limited, reared, as she had been, so apart from the world. Yet if she were ignorant in the accepted sense of the word, she must also be innocent, guileless, unacquainted with evil—white and unsullied in thought and experience. He had no desire for an intellectual wife; in his opinion the more women knew the more objectionable they became.

George Coventry was the kind of man who could contemplate matrimony only under conditions of supreme possession, mental as well as physical. What his wife learnt of life he must be the one to teach her; there must be no knowledge, no memory in her heart of which he might have reason to feel jealous in the most remote degree. There was something of the Sultan in his nature.

Perhaps he was not actively conscious of the stringency of his attitude towards the female sex; now, at least, he merely felt that he had "struck" the very kind of girl he should care to marry, and he harboured no manner of doubt in his mind but that Rafella Forte was all she appeared and all he conceived her to be—a sweet and simple creature, his ideal of a bride.

His instinct was not wrong. The vicar's daughter was a sweet and simple creature, oblivious, if not wholly ignorant, of evil—and of much besides. She made her own clothes, frequently she cleaned her own and her father's boots; she had driven in no vehicle more exalted than the village fly, had ridden nothing better than a donkey or a bicycle, had attended no entertainment more exciting than a local tea party or a penny reading. It was sinful, she thought, to powder one's nose, or to wear shoes with high heels, or to cut one's hair in a fringe—then a fashion that still was in favour. Her hats were kept on with elastic, and she seldom looked long at herself in the glass.

On the day of her sale, however, she looked at her reflection in the mirror rather more attentively than usual, just to make certain that her hair was as tidy as troublesome curls and waves would permit, that primrose soap and hot water had effectively cleaned her face after her busy morning, that her plain straw hat, bound by a white ribbon, and her linen collar were straight. She felt a trifle guilty because she desired to look her best, an ambition that was somehow entangled, quite unaccountably, with the prospect of meeting Captain Coventry again. She had never met anyone quite like Captain Coventry; he was so handsome and he seemed to be so nice. She looked forward with an odd and unwonted agitation to his arrival. She hoped, though she was teased by a slight suspicion to the contrary, that he was a *good* man, that he was a teetotaller, and did not smoke or play cards.

Then she went down into the garden, and became too deeply engrossed in the arrangement of her stall, and in consultations with early arrivals—the doctor's wife and the wives of one or two prominent farmers—as to the prices of their contributions, and at what time tea ought to be ready, and so forth, to concern herself further over his possible vices. She also forgot to consider his character when he drove up in a hired wagonette with his mother, a gracious old lady in black silk and a shawl, and his sister, a colourless person in a dust cloak, who might have been equally thirty or forty years of age. Rafella could think of nothing at the moment but the disturbing expression in Captain Coventry's eyes as he grasped her hand in greeting, his strong, brown face, his crisp moustache.

Further arrivals confused her, the schoolmaster and his family, parties of villagers, contingents from neighbouring parishes; she mixed up their names, could not confine her attention to their polite remarks; her usual calm self-assurance had fled, everything seemed curiously changed and unreal.

Coventry at once assumed the office of her chief assistant, and proved himself a valuable salesman. The women were attracted by his friendly manners and his good looks, the men were interested in his being a real soldier, in his having come from India. They called him "the Captain," and competed to have converse with him, even if it should entail the purchase of some useless article. His high spirits infected the company, and his marked attentions to the vicar's daughter caused general comment.

Rafella herself felt happy, extraordinarily elated; his open admiration gave her an unaccustomed sense of importance, and she was conscious of the notice it aroused. Animated, flushed, she looked a picture of exquisite maidenhood, in spite of her plain and homely toilet. In Coventry's eyes the virtuous simplicity of her attire only enhanced her charm. He felt he should hate to behold her in smart, up-to-date clothes.

The stall was soon cleared, and tea tickets sold well—sixpence a head for the affluent in the vicarage dining-room, twopence for the more humble out in the garden at a long trestle table in charge of the schoolmaster's wife. It was not until most of the throng had departed that Coventry found a chance of speaking with Rafella alone. He ignored the timid remarks of his sister concerning the time, her fears that "mother might feel fatigued or take cold if they remained too late"; and he calmly requested Miss Forte to show him the kitchen garden.

"There is not much to see, I'm afraid," Rafella said shyly, yet willing enough to take him.

"The very sight of an English kitchen garden is refreshing to anyone from India," he informed her; and they wandered off together, leaving Mr. Forte to entertain Mrs. Coventry and her daughter and one or two lingering visitors in the faded, old-fashioned drawing-room.

Truly there was little to see, beyond cabbages and gooseberry bushes, and the cherished potato patch, in the kitchen garden; the box borders had grown high and thick, and sadly needed trimming. There was an empty greenhouse, frequented by toads, and in one corner stood a shaky summer-house, suggestive of earwigs and spiders, dust and cobwebs.

But to Coventry it was a garden of glamour and dreams. For him a delicious enchantment hung in the air, an infinite pleasure pervaded his being; he wondered how long it must be before he might dare to proclaim his passion, before he might hold this dear girl in his arms as his promised wife.

"How would you like to go to India?" he asked her, dallying with the prospect of taking her there, visualising her bright presence in his bungalow.

"India! Oh, I don't know," she said, surprised. "I have never thought of going anywhere."

"But—but you will marry some day," he suggested tentatively, "and then you will have to go away."

She blushed and laughed a little nervously.

"Oh, that is not at all likely; and even if it were, how could I leave my father? He has become so dependent on me since my darling mother's death."

His spirits sank. He had forgotten all about her father, and the filial sense of duty that would, of course, prevail with such a dear, good girl. He resigned himself to the prospect of struggle, opposition; nevertheless, he meant to win, though in the end the marriage might have to be delayed for a reasonable period.

"But your father would never stand in the way of your happiness, surely?" he argued.

"I shouldn't be happy," she maintained, "if I thought I was behaving selfishly."

"Of course, to a certain extent you are right," he agreed; "but, after all, there are limits to unselfishness. Every woman has a just claim to her own existence." (In the case of his sister this view had not occurred to him.)

"Do you think so?" she asked doubtfully, in deference to his superior masculine wisdom.

"Yes, I do. And if you look a little farther, ought she to sacrifice the happiness of the man who loves her, in addition to her own?"

She blushed again, more deeply, and glanced away from him over the ragged garden steeped in the languorous peace of a summer sunset. "You see"—she hesitated—"I know nothing about—love." The word was spoken timidly, with modest reluctance.

"Sooner or later you are bound to learn its meaning," he said, controlling his impulse to declare that he would teach her. He recognised the risk of precipitancy; she must not be alarmed. As it was, she turned uneasily aside avoiding his gaze; said they ought to go back, it was getting late, Mrs. Coventry would be waiting for him; nervously polite little sentences.

In silence he followed her along the path that led to the door in the garden wall, noting the grace of her slender form, the glint of the curls that lay on her neck, the cream of the skin beneath the curls.

When they arrived at the door he said abruptly:

"I watched you go through here that morning. You had no hat on, and you were singing a hymn."

He was trying to close the door that was warped and stiff, so he missed the puzzled astonishment in her eyes.

"But how could you have seen me? It was ever so long before you came to the house."

"It was *why* I came to the house." He banged the door impatiently and faced her. "It was why I came *back*," he added with emphasis.

Colour flooded Rafella's face; he thought how adorably she blushed.

"Oh," she gasped; "but I thought it was because of a stone in your horse's shoe. Didn't you tell the truth?" she questioned severely.

He laughed, delighting in her naive sense of honesty. "There was a stone all right, I can assure you, and I blessed the excuse. All the same, I should have come back on some pretext or another. I could hardly have rung the front door bell and said I had observed a young lady with golden hair go through this door, and that I wanted to see her again. Now, could I?"

She turned away, confused, agitated, utterly unable to confront the tender banter in his eyes. But he had not quite done. As they went into the vicarage he asked boldly: "Can I come again, very soon, and talk to you in the garden?"

Though she made no answer he did not feel rebuffed.

Chapter 3

Success

Some three weeks later George Coventry proposed to Rafella Forte, but not among the roses in the sunshine, as he had so often pictured, for rain was coming down with inconsiderate persistence. The proposal took place in the church porch, where they lingered after choir practice, hoping it might clear.

His visits had been frequent since the day of the sale; and once he had persuaded the vicar and his daughter to spend an afternoon at his mother's house, conveying them to and fro at his own expense in the ever-available wagonette supplied by the country town inn.

To-day he had arrived just as Rafella was about to start for the church, enveloped in a macintosh, holding a monstrous cotton umbrella over her head; and for the last hour he had sat patiently in a pew while school children droned out hymns around Rafella and the harmonium, staring at him throughout the performance with unblinking curiosity.

Now the children had clattered away, Rafella had closed the harmonium and put everything straight, and they were alone in the porch; the church door, covered with notices, was closed behind them, and in front the rain streamed down on the huddled graves, the sunken, lichen-stained headstones, and the old-fashioned, coffin-shaped tombs.

The supreme moment had come when, in spite of the place and the weather, George Coventry felt he could be silent no longer. There was little doubt in his mind as to Rafella's feelings towards himself, there could be no doubt in hers as to his intentions; he had made them plain enough almost from the first.

It was very soon over. He had spoken, he had kissed her with passion yet reverence; she had trembled, shed a few tears, confessed that she cared for him. And then, as he had all along apprehended, came the protest, when he urged a short engagement, that she could not leave her father.

"It would be wicked of me to leave him by himself," she cried in tearful distress. "He could never get on without me. I think it would kill him, and I should never forgive myself."

"It would be wicked of *him* to want to keep you always," said Coventry firmly. He was prepared, within reason, to compromise, but he was also determined not to be beaten. "The moment we get back to the vicarage I'll interview him in his den. That was where you saw me first. Do you remember, little angel saint? You looked through the window, and I fell in love with your darling face, as I had already fallen in love with your hair and your voice. I say, couldn't we have that hymn at our wedding?

> *"'Other refuge have I none;*
> *Hangs my helpless soul on Thee.'"*

He sang the words joyfully, quite out of tune, for he was no musician.

"Oh, no. It wouldn't be suitable at all," she said, rebuke in her voice.

"I should say it was most appropriate, for I am going to comfort and protect you as long as I live."

"But it's not meant that way," she explained, shocked. "And, oh," she went on miserably, "you mustn't count on our being married. I feel dreadful about it all. I don't know *what* father would do without me. I can't think of going so far away and leaving him alone. Don't ask him; don't say anything about it."

Then, still standing in the porch, they went over it all again. He argued, entreated, cajoled, but her distress was so genuine, the conflict between her love and her duty so acute, that at last Coventry found himself willing, almost, to agree to an indefinite engagement, to the question of marriage being deferred till his next return from India. Finally he promised that if she would only give him permission to speak to her father he would press for no more than the vicar's consent to a wedding perhaps two years hence.

They returned to the house through the rain, Coventry rueful, depressed, yet alive to the virtue of Rafella's decision—it was only in accordance with the pure perfection of her character. He had little hope of Mr. Forte being equally unselfish, of his refusing to accept his daughter's temporary sacrifice; two years to a man of his age would seem a trifling period, and, of course, apart from personal inconvenience, he would be all in favour of discreet delay, and the wisdom of waiting, the test of time on the affections, and so forth. Coventry was conscious that were he in the vicar's place, with a young and guileless daughter to consider, his own sentiments would be identical; therefore he ultimately sought his future father-in-law's presence in a meek and dutifully acquiescent spirit, not altogether free from nervousness.

The vicar's mouldy sanctum was not quite the pleasant spot this afternoon that it had been on the occasion of Coventry's first visit; now the room was darkened by the rain, and the creepers, limp with moisture, clinging to the window. Mr. Forte himself looked dismal and depressed; he complained that the damp affected his throat and caused discomfort in his joints. He indicated with a weary gesture of his hand a pile of documents and ledgers connected with parish affairs, and some blank sheets of paper on which, owing to pressure of other business, his sermon for to-morrow had not yet been inscribed. He said he wished he could afford a curate, though to Coventry's consternation he affirmed that Rafella was as valuable to him as any curate could be, save in the matter of accounts and sermons.

"A good girl, Captain Coventry, a very good girl!" He shook his head as though he were saddened rather than cheered by the fact of Rafella's worth; but it was merely, as Coventry understood, the vicar's manner of emphasising his appreciation.

"Indeed, sir, she has no equal!" the younger man agreed with fervour.

It seemed a rather inauspicious moment for declaring his request, but delay could make no difference, and he spoke out boldly, though with quickened pulses, confessing that he had already approached Rafella and had not been rejected. To his amazed relief Mr. Forte listened to him with benign attention.

"I cannot pretend," he said, "that I have been altogether blind to your object in coming here, but before we go any farther there are one or two matters that must be discussed between us."

Coventry's heart went out to Rafella's father. He felt sure that the vicar was suppressing his own feelings in consideration of his cherished daughter's happiness.

"Dear old chap!" he thought warmly. Readily he said: "Of course—my prospects and my financial position, and my past? I hope I shall be able to satisfy you on every point." And he proceeded to explain that he possessed a fair income of his own apart from his pay, an income that must be materially increased on the death of his mother. Therefore he could make adequate provision for a wife and a possible family. There were no secrets in his past or his present; he had led a steady life, he was sound in health and, he hoped, in morals. As for religion, he was a member of the Church of England.

Then came a pause. Mr. Forte sat still, his elbow on the table, his head resting on his hand. He looked old and sad and tired, and George, with compunction, remembered his promise to Rafella.

"If you will give your consent to an engagement," he said impulsively, "I would undertake not to urge Rafella to marry me till I come back next time from India. I know she does not want to leave you yet, and it would be wrong and selfish of me to expect it."

The vicar placed his hand before his mouth and coughed. To Coventry his self-possession seemed extraordinary. The notion that worldly inducements might weigh with this simple old parson never came into his head.

"Well, well," said Mr. Forte magnanimously, "I must think it over. In the meantime, my dear lad"—with a smile of resignation he held out his hand and Coventry grasped it emotionally—"go and talk to Rafella."

He went, and a few minutes later the vicar resumed his spectacles, drew the blank sheets of sermon paper towards him, and opened his Bible. He happened to light upon the text:

"Discretion shall preserve thee, understanding shall keep thee."

And he began to write rapidly.

Mr. Forte had made up his mind that Rafella should marry Captain Coventry in the autumn and go back with him to India. He would miss his daughter sadly, the wrench of parting would be cruel, but such things had to be; God would give him grace to bear the trial. . . Otherwise, translated into the vulgar tongue—here was a young man of good character and safe position, with private means and clear prospects, who would make an excellent husband; it was a chance in a thousand, and if the fellow were ready and anxious to marry the penniless daughter of a poverty-stricken country clergyman, the vicar did not intend to discourage him nor to take the hazard of sentimental and unnecessary delays.

His decision was imparted (in the more dignified form) a couple of hours later to the expectant pair, whom he discovered seated close together on the springless sofa in the drawing-room, and there followed an affecting little scene. Tears, embraces, hand-shakes, blessings, assurances, general happy excitement, tinged for father and daughter with natural and touching melancholy.

When it was all over and the vicar had returned to his study, Coventry drew a long breath. The day for him had been one of unaccustomed emotional strain, and he felt a wholesome craving for refreshment.

Almost involuntarily he said: "I'd give anything for a peg!"

"A peg?" echoed Rafella, mystified.

"Meaning a whisky and soda."

"Oh, George!" She held primitive principles with regard to strong drink, though already she was reconciled to the fact that he smoked innumerable cigarettes.

"Is it so shocking?" he asked, with an indulgent smile.

"Well," she said uneasily, "you see, we think temperance so important. Beer I can understand, in strict moderation, though I don't approve of it; we always keep a small cask in the cupboard under the stairs in case it should be wanted, and, of course, there is a little brandy in my medicine chest; we use it, too, for moistening the jam papers. But we haven't any *whisky!*"

He perceived that the imbibing of spirits as an ordinary drink might appear to his fiancée as little less than wicked. Concealing his amusement, he explained, as a personal precaution, that though, of course, it was revolting to see a lady consume alcohol, unless by the doctor's orders, it was, taken judiciously, harmless, if not beneficial, to men, particularly to men accustomed to a hot climate; thus allaying her scruples and fears on his own behalf. He accepted a large cup of tea in preference to beer from the cupboard under the stairs, or brandy from the medicine chest, both of which Rafella proffered hospitably after his reassurance.

The wedding took place a fortnight before Coventry was to sail for India. One or two trivial disputes arose between the affianced pair, and on each occasion George's will prevailed. For example over the trousseau. It appeared that Rafella was entitled, on her twenty-first birthday, or on her marriage, to the legacy of a hundred pounds bequeathed to her by her godmother. She maintained that the half of this sum would be ample for her outfit, and she was on the point of engaging the village dressmaker to work daily at the vicarage, when George interfered. Though he did not wish Rafella to be anything but simply dressed, he had a suspicion that Under-edge fashions might be regarded as somewhat peculiar in an Indian military station. Therefore he insisted that her "costumes," as she called them, should at least be ordered in the little country town, under the guidance of his mother and sister, in whose taste he had implicit confidence. The result enchanted all concerned, though certainly it might have evoked contempt on the part of the more fastidious.

At any rate, in Coventry's eyes, and in the opinion of all present at the wedding, Rafella looked lovely as a bride; and, indeed, it was a very pretty ceremony, altogether, in its idyllic simplicity. The autumn day was radiant with sunshine, the kind of day when spiders' webs hang sparkling and perfect, as though spun with tiny crystal beads, and the air is still and humid; when the foliage, all red and gold, strikes wonder, and the blackberries are ripe and round and purple. The little church was decked with brilliant leaves and berries, and the pews were as well filled as if it had been Christmas Day. Not that any formal invitations had been issued; the only wedding guests from any distance were the bridegroom's near relations (he had few besides), and the bride's only aunt, who had consented to come and live at the vicarage and to join her small income to that of her brother. But the entire village was present in Sunday garments, save those who were bedridden and had been left without compunction to take care of themselves for the time. Rafella's only aunt did successful battle with the unwilling harmonium, and with much solemn emotion the vicar married his daughter to Captain Coventry.

It may be added that the bridegroom also had his way, after all, about the hymn, and it was sung by the congregation with a raucous fervour that stirred George Coventry to the depths of his being, for he could not help investing the words with a personal application, in spite of Rafella's previous protests to the contrary.

So the newly married pair sailed a fortnight later for India; and the unsophisticated daughter of an obscure country parson found herself launched without preparation into a world that to her was completely bewildering. From the stagnation of English village existence, and from relative hardship, she went straight into the activities, contradictions, and comparative luxuries of life in a large Indian station, a life that, perhaps, has no actual parallel anywhere else on earth.

Chapter 4

Mrs. Greaves

Mrs. Greaves stood on the platform of one of the largest railway stations in Upper India. The lights flashed down upon a pushing, shouting throng of dark-faced, turbaned humanity, for it was eight o'clock at night, and the mail train for Bombay was due to start in another few minutes. The chill, cold-weather mist of evening, creeping into the vast echoing station, seemed to compress the curious odours inseparable from an Eastern crowd—the sour exhalations, the commingling of spices and perfumes and garlic—and to prevent them from dispersing.

A little group of English people stood outside the door of a first-class compartment, a saloon-shaped compartment that to those unaccustomed to travel in the East would perhaps have seemed luxurious; but in a country where journeys may last for days and nights on end a certain degree of comfort becomes a necessity. Mrs. Greaves had come to the station to see Mrs. Munro, her friend, and little Trixie Munro, her godchild, off to England; also, incidentally, to take the bereft husband back to her bungalow for dinner with herself and Captain Greaves. It would be cruel, she felt, to permit the poor man to return to a lonely meal in the house that would still breathe of the presence of wife and child.

Within the compartment bedding had been laid out along the seats, luggage was heaped at one end—the loose, miscellaneous luggage of the Anglo-Indian traveller, brown canvas hold-alls, and clothes bags, sun hats, a tiffin basket, a water-bottle in a leather-case, and a lidless packing-case filled with odds and ends that might be needed on the journey down country. An ayah, enveloped in a scarlet shawl, was endeavouring to pacify the child, who, beside herself with excitement, was jumping up and down, and ordering her parents in shrill Hindustani to make haste and come inside the carriage, else they would assuredly be left behind. She had not understood as yet that Dadda must be left behind in any case.

At three years old little Trixie Munro was a beautiful baby, perfectly shaped, with masses of bright, curling hair, and luminous eyes; she was full of vitality, restless and gay as a sprite. Mrs. Greaves had always declared that Trixie looked as though she ought to be riding, naked, on a butterfly, with a little red cap on her head. She formed a striking contrast to her mother who, pale and tearful, almost in a condition of collapse, was nerving herself with trembling effort for her first parting from her husband, though she hoped he was to follow her on leave in six months' time. It is a very common scene in India, such partings on platforms or on steamer decks. Domestic separation is only a part of the price that is paid for service in the country, but it is a part that is by no means easy to bear, even when faced with submission and courage.

Mrs. Greaves's pleasant, freckled face was sad. She had been through such family partings herself, her own two robust little boys were at home, dedicated in the future to the Army and the Navy, and she sympathised with the husband and wife, neither of whom was very stout-hearted. Ellen Munro was her most intimate friend; it was a curious kind of friendship, based chiefly upon the fact that the two were old schoolfellows, and also distant connections. This had drawn them more closely together when they found themselves in the same station. But in character, as well as in looks, they were different—Marion Greaves being a sound and sensible little English memsahib, full of energy and common sense, with curling chestnut hair and a freckled skin that had earned her the good-natured nickname in the station of "The Plover's Egg." She loved riding and tennis and dancing, was fearless and direct. Whereas Ellen Munro was one of those helpless, incapable beings who seem to invite misfortune, and to accept it without a struggle. Her appearance was limp, her nature humble, affectionate, apologetic, and she clung with pathetic devotion to Marion Greaves, the staunchest of friends, who felt for her that species of protective fondness so often accorded to the weak by the strong. As for Mr. Munro, he was a delicate, clever young man, who would have been better at home in a Government office than leading the strenuous life of an Indian civilian. He could not handle a gun, he was never happy in the saddle, physically he soon tired, though his office work could not be beaten.

Mrs. Greaves frequently marvelled in secret how such a child as Trixie had ever been born of such parents—Trixie so vigorous, daring, self-willed, giving promise of a passionate, generous nature. She admired and loved her small goddaughter, and her affection for Ellen Munro, though tinged with contempt, was warm and sincere. Therefore she felt this good-bye acutely.

A sudden calm came over the hitherto noisy platform; passengers had at last been safely packed into the train, and arrivals had finally pushed and yelled themselves out of the station. One or two fruit and sweetmeat sellers, and a water-carrier, still wandered up and down with droning cries; and now the Munros got into the compartment together for a last embrace. Mrs. Greaves attracted Trixie to the window by holding up a toy she had brought with her for the purpose—that the child should not interrupt the parting. And while Trixie was laughing and chattering, and grabbing at her godmother's gift, her father kissed her swiftly; then, stepping white and silent from the carriage, he shut the door, and the train moved out of the station.

IT WAS VERY SOON AFTER Mrs. Munro had sailed for England that Rafella Coventry arrived in the station as a bride.

Mrs. Greaves saw her for the first time one afternoon seated a little apart, looking rather forlorn, watching her husband play tennis in the public gardens. The turf was emerald green, the blue, far-away sky was just flecked with some little white clouds that foretold the showers of winter; the air was crisp and exhilarating, and everyone save Mrs. Coventry was either playing a game, or awaiting their turns for tennis and badminton courts.

Rafella was suffering from a cold in her head, and her nose and eyes were inflamed. Deluded by the perpetual sunshine she had worn summer garments to start with, ignoring her husband's advice to the contrary; but now she sat wrapped in a cape that, though useful and warm, was unbecoming both in colour and style. She felt shy and depressed, and antagonistic towards this concourse of people, who all seemed to know one another so well—who belonged to a world that was completely outside her experience.

Mrs. Greaves asked who she was; and a malapert subaltern told her.

"That's the bride, Captain Coventry's new acquisition. Just the sort of raw rustic he would have chosen, with his peculiar ideas of what a woman should be. They say he discovered her in some prehistoric hamlet at home, and that she'd never seen a man till she met him, or a train till she started on her honeymoon. She looks like it. No fear of *her* kicking over the traces."

"You never know," laughed Mrs. Greaves. "And if you can forget her cape and her hat, and her obvious cold, you will observe that she is remarkably pretty, so you'd better reserve your judgment."

She had noted the beauty of the girl's eyes and complexion despite their present afflicted condition, and she guessed at the wealth of hair concealed by the unfashionable hat.

"An angel in asses' clothing—no, that's not quite right. What is the text exactly?"

"Oh! go and miss balls at tennis, and don't talk nonsense," advised Mrs. Greaves.

The woebegone appearance of the little bride had aroused her kind-hearted compassion. She approached Rafella, though they had not been introduced, and seated herself in a basket-chair at her side.

She began the acquaintance with the usual remarks and queries that greet all the newly arrived in India. Mrs. Coventry had never been out here before? What did she think of the country, of an Indian station? How did she like the life? What an extraordinary contrast it seemed at first, and so on.

"I remember so well," Mrs. Greaves chattered on in tactful sympathy, "how strange I found everything when I came out as a bride, though I was born in India and didn't go home until I was five. I made the most awful mistakes, and I thought I should never pick up Hindustani! I always said exactly the opposite to what I intended—like 'Come here' when I meant 'Go away'—which was so awkward if I happened to be in my bath!—and all that kind of thing."

Rafella's suspicions and shyness succumbed to these friendly advances. She confided to Mrs. Greaves that she was afraid she should find housekeeping dreadfully difficult—she had not been accustomed at home to an army of servants, nor to a lady's maid (as she called her ayah), nor to a carriage, nor to more than two courses at meals. It all seemed to her to savour of wicked display and extravagance; and as far as she could judge at present, people in India appeared to live for nothing but amusement and self-indulgence.

"But you must remember," admonished Mrs. Greaves, "that we are living under totally different conditions out here. The servants won't do each other's work, on account of their caste. We have to keep such a lot, not for our own convenience but for theirs. And you must have an ayah, unless you don't mind the menservants attending to your bedroom."

Rafella flushed uncomfortably. This last remark struck her as rather indelicate.

"Then as to the food," went on Mrs. Greaves, ignorant of having offended the taste of her hearer. "Materials are a good deal cheaper out here than they are at home, and not nearly so nourishing, so that extra courses in a climate like this are not so extravagant as they might seem. It is better to give the servants plenty to do, and to keep them up to a certain standard, since we have to respect their prejudices; and there is also custom and prestige to be considered, which are not to be slighted in this country. That you will soon find out! If you were to reduce your establishment and your meals, and your general manner of living in your position, you'd never get a respectable servant to stay with you, and your name would be a byword in the bazaar!"

There was a pause. Rafella said nothing, and Mrs. Greaves felt she had come up against a narrow and obstinate nature. Nevertheless, she continued her well-meant harangue.

"As to amusements, what else have we to fall back upon but each other's society? We are all cut off from home and our relations and intellectual advantages; and wholesome exercise, whether tennis, riding, dancing, or sport, cannot be classed as self-indulgence when it is well within our reach financially. The men work hard for the greater part of the day—perhaps you have not yet realised how much your husband gets through before he is free to follow the recreations that suit him best? You mustn't judge Indian life too quickly from the surface, or from your own standpoint."

"I wish to do good," said Rafella priggishly, "and it seems to me that I have no one to be kind to but the ayah."

"Don't worry about that!" advised Mrs. Greaves, suppressing a smile. "There's plenty of time. You'll find you'll have as much as you can do for the next few months getting used to India, and, if I may make a suggestion, don't be *too* kind to the ayah, or she'll think you're afraid of her and take every advantage. What native servants appreciate is justice and patience, not indulgence, which they always mistake for weakness."

"She certainly has asked for a great many things," Rafella confessed, "but she seems so poor, and says she has such a large family, that I gave her more wages and some clothes, and a very nice lantern and a couple of warm blankets, and I have promised her an allowance of sugar and tea and the money to buy a goat."

"Well, I hope you won't regret it," remarked Mrs. Greaves.

"Have you ever regretted doing what you could for other people?" There was lofty reproach in Mrs. Coventry's voice.

"Often!" replied Mrs. Greaves, unashamed.

Despite this admission, she did all she could for Mrs. Coventry during the next few weeks, having regard to the bride's youth and inexperience, for the colonel of Captain Coventry's regiment was a bachelor, and just then, as it happened, there were no other ladies with the battalion. She was rather missing Ellen Munro, and was glad to transfer her support and counsel to Rafella Coventry, imparting to her all she knew herself concerning household management in India and Anglo-Indian rules and customs. All about calling and precedence, and dusters and charcoal, and stores and prices, including the error of supposing that a memsahib need never go near her kitchen, or bother about the milk and the water, and pots and pans, "for," she cautioned her pupil, "that way typhoid lies!"

Thus she came to know Mrs. Coventry rather well, though at the bottom of her heart she was reluctantly aware that she would never grow really attached to this Madonna-faced young woman who so prided herself on her conscience, and was so severe on the failings of others. She was called "sweet little Mrs. Coventry" by the station when her cold had subsided, for her beauty, combined with her puritanical notions, formed a novel attraction. As time went on she learnt to ride, and play tennis after a fashion, also to dance quite nicely, in order, as she carefully explained, to please her husband; but as George Coventry did not dance, and openly preferred racquets to tennis, and pig-sticking and polo to aimless rides, the excuse seemed a trifle superfluous. At the same time, everyone agreed that however indifferently she might ride or play tennis, her husband ought more often to share with her both forms of exercise.

These active accomplishments were taught her for the most part by admiring subalterns, who raved of her hair and her eyes and her seraphic disposition. Later, Mrs. Greaves was amused to observe that Rafella was making efforts to arrange her hair in the latest fashion. Her hair, she told Mrs. Greaves, was coming out in handfuls, and she thought a change for a time might prove beneficial. Then the mud-coloured dresses and high evening gowns were gradually discarded, to be replaced by white linens and serges, and simple though elegant frocks for dinners and dances. Also, there came a gradual moderation in Mrs. Coventry's opinions, a setting aside of small scruples, significant signs of a self-confident conceit that was fostered by the opportunities and circumstances inseparable from a mode of life in direct opposition to the one in which she had been reared. The ayah found herself neglected; Rafella had discovered a pleasanter method of doing good to others, that of bestowing good advice on erring young men, inviting their confidences, using her pure and virtuous influence—deluding herself and the susceptible youths with the notion that she was their mother-confessor and friend, their safeguard against the wicked temptations and wiles of the world. In short, though with the

ALICE PERRIN

most innocent motives, "sweet little Mrs. Coventry" got herself talked about, for these secrets entailed prolonged consultations, seclusion in corners apart from the crowd, notes, and mysterious appointments.

At first Captain Coventry laughed and paid little attention. Rafella kept nothing from him. He heard the whole history of Mr. Ricardo's engagement, that was such a mistake, to a girl he had ceased to care for at home. He knew all about Dickie Macpherson's dreadful entanglement, that he now so bitterly repented, with an unscrupulous woman; and he pretended to listen to all that Rafella had preached to young Grey so successfully on the subject of cards and champagne.

Mrs. Greaves wondered how long it would be before he awoke to the fact that his wife was indulging in pious flirtations that were regarded by the station with good-natured amusement.

One afternoon she was astonished to meet Rafella riding demurely along the Mall with Mr. Kennard. The man was a barrister, handsome, successful, in the prime of his maturity, but his moral reputation was anything but good. If Rafella had schemes for reforming this gentleman, serious trouble would certainly follow. George Coventry was hardly the man to look on and laugh at a dangerous friendship; Rafella's little team of harmless young men was a different matter altogether.

Mrs. Greaves's expression as she returned their salutations must have betrayed her surprised apprehension, for Rafella flushed as she nodded, and Mr. Kennard smiled with sardonic understanding.

"Evidently that woman thinks I'm not a fit companion for you," he said to Rafella as they rode on beneath the trees. "She's always had her knife into me, though she poses as a model of charity and soft-heartedness. What a pity it is when lemon juice is blended with the milk of human kindness! I don't know why she should try to do me harm, unless it's because I have never gone out of my way to propitiate her; but, then," he added with flattering emphasis, "there are very few women I care to make friends with."

Rafella felt that this was not what she should have expected of Mrs. Greaves. It only showed how mistaken one might be in one's estimate of other people's natures. She answered sympathetically:

"How narrow-minded of her. I shouldn't pay any attention to what she thought or said."

"I don't," he assured her; "and may I say that I hope you won't either?"

He reined his horse a little closer to Rafella's and looked into her eyes with subtle appeal.

"Of course I shouldn't," she said, returning his gaze with innocent encouragement. "I always take people as I find them, and I never listen to gossip."

He just touched her arm with his own in grateful appreciation. "That's a relief to my mind," he told her. "You don't know how hard it is to live down indiscretions, even when they may not have been all one's own fault. Some day, if you will let me, I should like to tell you a lot about myself, though there is no reason why I should bother you with my affairs."

Rafella's heart went out to him. All the little confidences of her boy admirers seemed trivial in comparison with the unfortunate experiences of this man of the world. She was well aware that he was ill-spoken of by the more scrupulous members of the community; but she felt convinced he was misjudged, and even if there should be truth in such reports as she had heard, surely sympathy and kindness from a woman who was good was all he needed to enable him to make amends for everything, however regrettable, that might have happened in the past.

It was only during the last ten days that Mr. Kennard had sought Mrs. Coventry's company. As a rule he consorted chiefly with the "smarter" portion of society in the station, the English cavalry regiment, and a few pretentious people with private incomes, who affected to order their households on lines that were more or less English, and to despise what they called "country ways." Sometimes the result of such pretension was ludicrous, but, on the whole, the humble outsider was deeply impressed, while the envious raged and scorned. Such a clique concerned themselves little with anyone's morals, provided their guests were as exclusive as themselves and could afford to return their festivities. It was a feeble reflection of a second-rate section of London society.

Mr. Kennard began his campaign by calling on Mrs. Coventry, without, however, the smallest apology for never having done so before, though the Coventrys lived in the bungalow next to his own. It must be confessed that Rafella, instead of receiving him coldly, or not receiving him at all, felt gratified rather than ruffled by this belated attention, though she condemned the circle in which he moved.

She told George of the visit with ill-concealed triumph. She knew there were several women who were anxious for Mr. Kennard to call on them, who even had lowered themselves so far as to send him invitations to dinner, which for the most part he did not trouble to answer. Rafella felt she had scored. But George did not share her elation.

"That fellow!" he said contemptuously. "What infernal cheek. Don't let him hang about this house, that's all."

"But, surely," argued Rafella in gentle reproach, "it would be better for him to come here if it takes him away from the frivolous people he mixes with now?"

"Birds of a feather," said George. "He's a beast, and I hate him."

George seemed in such a bad temper to-day that she considered it wiser at present to withhold the information that she had told Mr. Kennard he might come in and see her whenever he liked. Sometimes George was so hard and intolerant. She wished he was rather more Christian in his ideas. She made up her mind that if Mr. Kennard could be weaned from his bad companions it was her duty to undertake such a good work, and George would be wrong to hinder her efforts.

Mr. Kennard very soon came again, and she felt rather relieved that he should have chosen a time when George was absent on duty. They strolled round the garden and talked of things in the abstract. Rafella was gracious and kind, and looked sweet in her soft white gown and flower-trimmed hat. Mr. Kennard was delightful, she thought. His manner was so courteous and charming, and he listened with such deferential respect to anything she had to say. Evidently he felt it a privilege to be in her company. Once or twice he just touched on his loneliness as a bachelor, which drove him, he hinted, to seek undesirable distractions—distractions of which, in his heart, he was weary and sometimes ashamed. It was all very subtly conveyed, and Rafella felt more than ever convinced that he needed most sorely the friendship and help of a high-minded woman, and that she was the woman to provide what was wanted. He must have been "guided" to come to her, and she prayed for him hard that night.

The visits continued. Sometimes she mentioned to George that Mr. Kennard had looked in to lend her a book, or to leave her a bunch of his violets—he was famous for his violets, that bloomed in pots three deep in his veranda. More often she held her tongue; not that she had any feeling of guilt in the matter, but because George was unreasonable about Mr. Kennard. He had taken to sulking whenever he saw the man at her side in the club or in the gardens, and was cross if she danced with him more often than once, or if he joined her out riding.

She was perfectly aware that George did not suspect her of anything wrong; it was Mr. Kennard he suspected; and on one occasion, when he had been almost violent because Mr. Kennard had given her a dog, she spoke her mind, calmly, persuasively, pointing out that Mr. Kennard always behaved like a gentleman, that George was not treating her fairly by making such scenes, and that he could not know how deeply her feelings were hurt.

Then she broke down and cried like a child that is punished unjustly; and George took her in his arms and kissed her, trying to feel that he had been a brute, knowing all the time that his instinct was correct, that Kennard was not the right man for his wife to befriend.

Chapter 5

The Lie

Rafella took rather unfair advantage of George's repentance, undoubtedly half-hearted though it was. She asked him, as she forgave him, if he would not try to be generous, and allow her to invite Mr. Kennard to dinner, only to show that he realised the unreasonableness of his attitude? And with her golden head on his shoulder, and her soft lips close to his own, Coventry consented.

As might have been expected the experiment was not a success. Even before dinner was over Rafella perceived her mistake. She had hoped so much from the evening—hoped that her husband and Mr. Kennard would make friends, that in future all would be pleasant and smooth.

Instead of which George broke his promise, and behaved like a bear. He was a man who could not conceal his aversions, and seldom attempted to do so; and the mere sight of Mr. Kennard at his table, sleek and urbane, and indifferent to his dislike, incensed him and rendered him glum and ungracious. He talked, when he talked at all, only to Mrs. Greaves, who, with her husband and Mr. Munro, made up the party of six. Mrs. Greaves saw with foreboding the look in George Coventry's eyes as he watched his wife and Mr. Kennard conversing with intimate ease, and she felt as if they were eating their dinner with an explosive beneath the table. How she wished Rafella were not such a self-confident fool! Since the day on which she had met the pair riding together Rafella had carefully avoided being alone with her; she hoped when they repaired to the drawing-room that she might have a chance of introducing a word of advice, but whether by intention or otherwise the *tête-à-tête* was evaded; coffee was served in the dining-room, and later they all left the table together.

Mrs. Coventry preserved a semblance of good spirits during the uncomfortable hour that followed. She warbled a few English ballads while her husband scowled in a corner and Mr. Kennard turned over the songs for his hostess. He alone of the company appeared quite unaffected by the strain in the atmosphere.

Mrs. Greaves rose early to go, and Mr. Munro escaped simultaneously. As they drove out of the compound, Mrs. Greaves said to her husband:

"What an appalling evening! I can't think how Rafella persuaded her husband to let her invite that odious man. Evidently he did it under protest. I only hope he didn't look back into the drawing-room when he was seeing us off."

Mrs. Greaves, looking back, had observed Mr. Kennard bending over Rafella at the piano, obviously uttering words that caused her to lower her head in self-conscious confusion.

"I'm certain," Mrs. Greaves added, "he was taking the opportunity when our backs were turned of saying something he shouldn't."

"Well, it's no business of ours," said Captain Greaves, with masculine unconcern. "Kennard's a rascal, and the woman's an ass, as I've always told you; and if Coventry can't manage his wife it's his own fault. Anyway, you can do nothing to stop it, so you'd better not interfere."

"But I shall interfere," said his wife. "I can't see Rafella wrecking her happiness, and not say a word."

Captain Greaves only shrugged his shoulders and urged the pony along.

What Mr. Kennard had been saying to Rafella, when her husband had left the room, was this:

"I'm afraid I did wrong to come. I hope it won't mean a bad time for you afterwards?"

"I—I hoped it would have been all right," Rafella faltered, gazing down at the keys of the piano.

He sighed. "Give a dog a bad name," he quoted despairingly. "In future I suppose I'd better keep away. It would be wiser for your sake. I'd do anything to save you bother and prevent misunderstandings. I should be the only one to suffer, and I dare say I deserve it."

"Oh, I am so sorry! I can't tell you how sorry and ashamed I feel." Her eyes were full of tears as she raised them to his for a moment.

"You know you've only to tell me what you want me to do, and I'll do it, Rafella."

"Hush!" she said tremulously. "If you talk like that, I shall be obliged to tell you to keep away."

"Would you miss me—would you mind if you never saw me again?" Before she could answer, he raised his voice. "And so you see there was nothing else to be done," he said cheerfully, for Coventry had re-entered the room.

Mr. Kennard accepted a drink offered with curtness by his host, and then he went back to his bungalow.

ALICE PERRIN

Rafella tidied her music in offended silence. She felt very angry with George. He had behaved so rudely and spoilt the evening, and she meant him to feel her displeasure. George also was silent, provokingly silent; he smoked a cigarette and drank a whisky and soda, and did not appear to be conscious of her annoyance. At last she threw down a volume of songs with a bang on the piano, and burst into tears. To her astonished resentment George took no notice. It was the first time since their marriage that her tears had not melted his heart. In a passion of mortification she rushed from the room. With her usual self-righteous consideration she never exacted her ayah's attendance the last thing at night, so there was no need to check her distress in her bedroom. Still crying she quickly undressed and got into bed, and then she lay waiting for George to come in and say he was sorry, to own himself in the wrong.

She could hear him moving about in his dressing-room. Several times she was tempted to call him, but pride held her dumb, so convinced did she feel that he owed her amends for his conduct, that the first advances should come from him. But she waited in vain. George remained in his room; and Rafella, exhausted with tears and emotion, finally fell asleep.

When she awoke in the morning, later than usual, she was told that the sahib had gone forth at daybreak to shoot, and had left her a message to say that he should not return till the evening. Often when George had arranged to take a day's shooting, he slept in his dressing-room so that he should not disturb Rafella by rising at dawn, and it was rather a relief to feel that the present occasion would give rise to no comment among the servants. She remembered that to-night he was dining at mess, and she determined rancorously that she would not be in to receive him when he came home to dress.

Before she was out of her room a note and a book and a posy of violets came from Mr. Kennard. She replied to the note with a smile of bitter complacency curving her lips.

That evening Mrs. Greaves turned over the pages of a fashion paper in a corner of the club. It was previous to the days when "going to the club" had ceased to be a popular proceeding; it was not yet considered more civilised to go home with a few particular friends for the interval before dinner. The ladies' room was filled with groups of people refreshing themselves with tea after healthy exercise afoot or on horseback, or on the river, and the lofty building resounded with voices and laughter. The hot weather was within measurable distance, but the days were still pleasant, and the general exodus to the hills had not begun. The tennis courts in the public gardens were crowded every evening, the bandstand well surrounded, the Mall lively with riders and drivers; and the last ball of the season had yet to take place.

Mrs. Greaves had played four sets of tennis, and now she was waiting for her husband to join her from the polo ground.

Two women seated themselves at a tea-table just in front of her, and though she was absorbed in making up her mind whether to send home for one of the seductive blouses sketched on the advertisement page of the paper, she heard, unavoidably, scraps of their talk. First they discussed the ball that the bachelors of the station were giving next night in return for hospitality extended to them throughout the cold weather by the married members of the community. It was, they believed, to be an exceptionally brilliant affair; the supper was to include pomfrets from Bombay, and confections from Peliti's—the Buszard of India. From this they went on to the subject of their gowns for the ball.

Then one of them said: "Look! There's Mrs. Coventry, and, needless to say, Mr. Kennard."

The other looked up sharply; so did Mrs. Greaves, and this was the conversation that reached her unwilling ears.

"Did you ever see such a change in anyone? You weren't here when she came out as a bride? No, of course, I remember, you were at home. I assure you she looked like a Salvation Army lass, or a charity school girl, her hair dragged back in a knob like a door-handle, and *hideous* clothes. She would hardly speak to a man, and was horrified at everything and everybody. And now behold her, with a fringe, and dressed as well as anyone in the place, and, of all men, the irresistible Mr. Kennard in attendance. The boys' brigade appears to have been disbanded in his favour. He likes the field to himself."

"What will be the end of it, do you think?"

The other shrugged her shoulders. "What has been the end of all his affairs with women? Scandal and unpleasantness for them, and certainly, in one instance at least, disgrace and divorce, while he has gone scot free. He was notorious before he came here from the Punjaub, and yet he goes on as if nothing had happened. Some people run after him because he's a rich barrister and can entertain, and gives himself airs. Look at that little idiot over there, hanging on his every word. Her husband would be furious. I dare say he'll be here in a minute, and then we shall see."

Mrs. Greaves left her seat. She intended that these "tattle-snakes," as she dubbed all scandalmongers, should suffer disappointment. If she could help it there should be no thrilling little scene for them to witness with malevolent enjoyment. Deliberately she made her way across the room towards the couple under observation.

Mr. Kennard rose at once and gave her his chair, drawing another one forward for himself. He looked very handsome, very self-contained; even Mrs. Greaves was grudgingly conscious of his attraction, much as she distrusted and disliked him.

"Rafella," she began in plausible entreaty, "could you possibly give me a lift home? My old man has evidently forgotten that he was to pick me up on his way back from polo, and we've people coming to dinner. I shall hardly have time to make the salad and put out the dessert!"

Mrs. Coventry hesitated perceptibly. She looked at Mr. Kennard, who did not return her glance. His face was blandly impassive.

"Are you waiting for your husband?" inquired Mrs. Greaves. "If so, perhaps Mr. Kennard would drive me home." She hoped with fervour that her own husband would not arrive inconveniently, before she could complete her manoeuvre.

Mrs. Greaves, remembering that Mr. Kennard's bungalow was next door to that of the Coventrys, felt more than ever determined to lure Rafella away, and to take the opportunity of speaking her mind. She, of course, could not know that Mrs. Coventry had intended to remain at the club till her husband must have started for the mess. She was only aware that Rafella was reluctant to leave.

"Oh, then," she said cheerfully, "that's all right. Would you mind if we started at once?" She turned to Mr. Kennard. "If my husband should turn up after all, would you tell him I've gone? It will serve him right for being so late."

Presently the two women were driving swiftly along the broad road that led from the club to the native cavalry lines. Mrs. Greaves kept up a desultory flow of small talk until they arrived at the steps of the veranda. Then she said urgently: "Rafella, I want you to come in for a moment."

"But you'll be busy."

"No, I shan't. Look here, Rafella, we haven't anybody dining with us, and Jim hadn't forgotten to call for me. He's probably at the club now, and when he finds I've gone home, he'll stay and play billiards, or something, for a bit. I perjured myself on your account, and I want you to come in and hear why I did it."

Unwillingly, and with an air of offended mystification, Mrs. Coventry complied.

"What on earth do you mean?" she inquired once they were inside the comfortable drawing-room. "How could you tell me such dreadful untruths?"

She stood, looking disturbed and suspicious, in the yellow lamplight, while Mrs. Greaves shook up the fat cushions on the sofa and pushed her gently in among them. Then she explained. She repeated part of the conversation she had overheard at the club, she expressed her own opinion of Mr. Kennard, and she told Mrs. Coventry in plain words that she was making a fool of herself.

Flushed and indignant, Rafella sprang up from the nest of cushions.

"It's intolerable!" she cried. "I won't listen. You are every bit as bad as those two poisonous women you overheard talking. Your mind must be as evil as theirs. I tell you there is no harm in my friendship with Mr. Kennard; he has been awfully kind to me, sending me flowers and lending me books, and I hope I have been of some help to him; he is grateful, that is all."

"His gratitude will be mistaken by other people for something not quite so harmless," warned Mrs. Greaves; and Rafella did feel a little disturbed in her conscience as she remembered the tone of his voice and his use of her Christian name on the previous night. But she assured herself George was to blame, indirectly, for that; Mr. Kennard had forgotten himself at the moment only because he felt so indignant with George for his conduct towards her. It was simply an outburst of chivalrous sympathy, though, of course, she would never permit it to happen again.

Marion Greaves was still talking. "As long as you only played about with a lot of nice, harmless boys, I knew you were safe enough; but the moment this man began to single you out——"

"I have never 'played about,' as you vulgarly put it," interrupted Rafella furiously. "The boys are just like brothers to me. They miss their women relations at home, and I can give them advice, and listen to their troubles, and often help them very much. They know I don't want them to make love to me, and that I wouldn't allow such a thing!"

"If you were old and plain, they wouldn't ask for your help and advice. But that is beside the point. We are talking now about Mr. Kennard."

"And I tell you again there is no harm in our friendship, and as long as my conscience is clear the friendship will continue."

"You know your husband hates him," said Mrs. Greaves bluntly, "so your conscience can't be completely clear."

The flush died away from Rafella's cheeks; she twisted her fingers together, and her voice shook as she answered defiantly: "He should be the last person to misjudge me, or to put a wrong construction on my friendships."

Mrs. Greaves wished to goodness the girl would break down and cry, then she might be more easy to manage. But there she stood, pale and pig-headed, so *silly*, and the other woman longed to shake her. Of course the little fool was flattered by the man's attentions, fatally attracted by his arts and wiles, and with a husband like Coventry, who had always been hard on the frailties of women, intolerant even of harmless flirtation, there was bound to be serious trouble sooner or later. What was to be done!

Mrs. Greaves struggled to keep her temper. "Well, my dear," she urged gently, "all I can say is that you'd better be careful. Mr. Kennard's friendships with other men's wives have never yet been regarded as blameless! And I ask you—is it worth the risk of a row with your husband? Wouldn't it be wiser to quarrel with Mr. Kennard than with the man you must live with for the rest of your life?"

Even Rafella could hardly deny the plain common sense of this pleading. She evaded the question, repeated that she had done nothing unworthy, and said that if George could not trust her——

"Oh, good heavens!" Mrs. Greaves broke in wearily. "Of course George trusts you. But he can't bear you to be talked about, and you ought to consider his feelings. Anyone can see you are making him jealous. Those women in the club this evening were thirsting for him to come in and find you sitting alone with Mr. Kennard."

"India is a wicked place!" cried Rafella; "full of gossips and scandalmongers and evil-minded people. Why can't they leave one alone?"

"My good girl, India is no worse than any other part of the globe that is inhabited by human beings," argued Mrs. Greaves; "but out here we are all necessarily thrown a great deal together, and women of our class associate with men much more than is usual or possible for us to do at home. If we are sensible it does us and the men no manner of harm, rather the reverse. If we are fools it may turn our heads, and then, of course, the men will amuse themselves accordingly."

"My head is not turned," said Rafella, like a child; and with an effort Mrs. Greaves forbore to contradict her. It was clear that nothing further could be said at present without endangering their friendship, which for Rafella's sake was not to be desired.

"Well, don't let us argue about it any more. We'll drop the subject. And do stay and dine with us, as your husband is out to-night and you're alone."

"No, thank you," refused Rafella with stiff politeness; and she went to the door.

Persuasion failed to move her, and with a kindly, regretful "good-night" Mrs. Greaves watched her climb into her trap and drive away. She had an uneasy suspicion that Rafella's determined refusal was due not so much to her outraged feelings as to either the hope, or the certainty, that Mr. Kennard would come over to see her during the evening.

Rafella wept when she got home. She felt like a persecuted Christian, and she could not touch her solitary meal. It was true that her conscience was clear of wrongdoing and of any attempt to deceive. The differences between herself and her husband regarding her innocent "friendship" had, of course, been very distressing, but George was to blame; he was entirely in the wrong. She considered that instead of being cross and disagreeable, George ought to encourage her to exercise her influence for good, especially with a man like Mr. Kennard, if all that was said of him was true—which she did not believe. George's hostility towards Mr. Kennard had aroused all the obstinacy in her nature. Her self-esteem was wounded. It was positively insulting of George to question her conduct. She might as well suspect him of gambling because he played cards, or of drinking because he was not a teetotaller. Whatever George, or Mrs. Greaves, or anyone else might say, she was not going to treat Mr. Kennard as though he were a scoundrel, nor to behave as if she had done wrong herself. Why should she forgo the pleasure of his society, and why should she deprive him of her sympathy and her friendship, which she knew was of comfort and help to him, merely because a few spiteful people chose to see evil where no evil existed?

After pretending to eat her dinner, she lay on the sofa and tried to read one of the books Mr. Kennard had lent her. It was called "Degeneration," and she found it very difficult to follow; still, he had told her that she ought to take an interest in every phase of human nature, and she plodded through the first few pages. She soon found that she could not fix her attention. As a matter of fact, the subject of the book was beyond her simple understanding; and, in addition, she was listening, subconsciously, for footsteps in the veranda.

At last she rose and wandered out into the garden, feeling very lonely, very much aggrieved. Self-pity overwhelmed her. Looking back upon the period that had passed since her arrival as a bride in India, so eager, so happy, so filled with faith in the future, it all seemed to her like a long and exhausting dream; and now she was conscious of nothing but doubt, disillusion, and righteous indignation.

And, indeed, the whole machinery of Rafella's mental outlook was deranged and dislocated. Her perceptions had been weakened by the effort to adjust her mind to unaccustomed circumstances, and she mistook her own failure to resist deterioration for a sort of jealous plot on the part of other people to undermine her judgment and her purity of purpose.

She paced the patch of drive that showed ghostly and grey in the starlight. Through the thin screen of oleander trees that, with a low mud barrier, divided the Coventrys' compound from the compound of their neighbour Mr. Kennard, she could see the lights of his bungalow. She thought of him with tenderness as one who, like herself, was a victim of the little-minded. The voluptuous warmth and peace of the night soothed her over-excited nerves. . . She wished that Mr. Kennard would come over and talk to her. She had felt so confident that he would come, if only for just a few minutes, knowing that she was alone. A little breeze caressed her face in soft, warm waves; as she paused beneath the trees they seemed to lean towards her in the darkness with whispers of support and consolation. The furtive noises of the Indian night did not alarm her—a rustle in the undergrowth, the sudden flapping of a flying fox, the flitter of a bat, the distant squealing of some helpless little creature in the agonies of capture by a foe. She went on, as in a dream, until she reached the gateless entrance of the compound, where she paused, standing in the loose white dust that still retained the heat of the day. An ekka passed, with jingling bells, along the road outside, then a creaking cart close-packed with pilgrims on their journey to some sacred shrine, chanting sleepily a song of prayer and praise. Silent-footed travellers, enshrouded in their cotton sheets, slipped by and disappeared like wraiths.

"Mrs. Coventry—is that you?"

Involuntarily she started, though she knew she did not feel surprised. Kennard had come out of his gate, and was standing at her side; she had not heard his footsteps in the dust. His figure, in the starlight, looked black and indistinct, save for his white shirt-front and the burning end of his cigar. It suddenly struck Rafella that, since she had known

Mr. Kennard, the odour of strong cigars was no longer repugnant to her—she who had always detested the smell of tobacco, who had never grown really accustomed to George's innumerable cigarettes! Vaguely she wondered why this should be, as he stood talking—talking, she noticed, as superficially as if they had been in a room full of listening people—about the warmth of the night and the approaching hot weather, and how difficult it was to settle down to a book or anything else in a stuffy bungalow after dinner, with mosquitoes biting one's ankles, etc. Rafella appreciated the delicacy of his attitude; she thought it exceedingly nice of him not to attempt to take any advantage of the situation. And yet if George were to see them together now, he would straightway assume that Mr. Kennard was making love to her, and that she was allowing him to do so!

The thought of her husband gave her a feeling of uneasiness. She did not know how long it was since she had left the house; it might have been equally hours or minutes ago as far as she was concerned; George might return any moment and discover her here by the road in the darkness with Mr. Kennard, and of course he would never believe——

She said: "I think I had better go back." Yet still she lingered, captive to the magic of the night, and the heavy scent of blossoms mingling with the fumes of his cheroot; held, also, by the lurement of his presence, and a novel sense of high adventure.

"You know you ought not to come out at night without a lantern," he told her. "It's just the time of year when snakes begin to lie about in the dust and are still half-torpid from the winter."

"Then why did *you* come out without a lantern?" she asked, picking up her skirts a little anxiously.

At first he did not answer. Then he said: "Perhaps I'd better not explain." He paused. "After all," he added, "I don't see why I shouldn't tell you. The truth is I just felt I *must* come and stand at your gate, and I forgot all about lanterns and snakes."

"Why couldn't you have come over, lantern and all, after dinner for a chat?"

She would not recognise his meaning, thrilled though she was by his homage.

"I knew you were alone. Would it have been wise?"

"Well, perhaps not," she agreed, "and it's also not wise for us to stay talking here in the dark with snakes all over the place; I must go in. Good-night, Mr. Kennard."

He held her hand. "You'll keep me some dances to-morrow night, won't you? I'm one of your hosts, remember. Promise you won't disappoint me?"

"Of course not," she promised him gently, withdrawing her hand.

He hesitated. "I think I'll just see you as far as the steps of the veranda. I should feel more comfortable. I can go back by the gap in the boundary—where it's broken, you know."

She knew. He had often come over that way in the daytime.

They strolled to the veranda steps in silence; then again they said "Good-night," and Kennard vanished swiftly in the darkness.

"Won't you borrow one of our lanterns?" she called after him, remembering with horror the danger of snakes.

There came no answer, for at that moment Rafella's husband drove in at the gate.

"Were you calling to someone?" he inquired, with surly suspicion, as he joined her in the veranda.

For the first time in her life Rafella told a deliberate lie. "No," she said, her heart fluttering painfully with fear and shame. "I had only just come out to listen for the trap."

Chapter 6

THE BACHELORS' BALL

T he rhythm of the immortal "Blue Danube" waltz swung through the big Indian ballroom. It was long before two-steps, Bostons, tangos were dreamed of, when, at any rate in India, the *pas de quatre* was still a novelty, and the "Washington Post" had not yet been introduced. Almost everyone was dancing; the only onlookers were a few partnerless, or non-dancing men, and a sprinkling of senior people whose exile in the East was nearly over. The aged white man or woman is seldom to be encountered in India; they have "done their time" and gone home—or to their graves. Sometimes they stay to live out last years in some more or less salubrious region, but such settlers are dying out, and, with easier transit home, are not replaced; for though living may be less expensive, and cheap luxuries attractive, there is always the loss of prestige and the desire to end their days in England.

There seemed no doubt that the final ball of the cold weather season was a triumphant success. The bachelor hosts had spared neither effort nor money to perfect every arrangement, from the par excellent supper upstairs to the most trifling detail below. The compound of the public building was illuminated with row upon row of little lights in coloured glass receptacles, verandas were enclosed and decorated, tents were added too, carpeted and furnished, for the benefit of sitters-out; plants were in profusion, flowers, Chinese lanterns, casual buffets for promiscuous refreshment—nothing was forgotten.

Every girl had partners, the programmes of the more popular spinsters had been filled for days, and usually hopeless wallflowers were not allowed to sit neglected as long as a man who could dance was unwary enough to remain unattached in the ballroom. Even the most unattractive of the three Miss Planes ("Plain," "Plainer," "Plainest," as they were called by irreverent subalterns) had been dancing all night, and as a result of enjoyment looked almost attractive.

Among the non-dancing men was Captain Coventry; entertainments of this description bored him unutterably. Polo and sport were his recreations, and he could not and would not dance; it was a form of amusement he held in contempt. To-night he felt more disinclined than usual to make himself useful or pleasant. Sullen and solitary, he leaned against the wall in gloomy contrast with the gay festoons of muslin, blue and white and yellow, draped behind him. He was a man not seen at his best in a ballroom, and just at that moment he appeared at his worst, for his wife had danced four times already with the man he most loathed in the station, and again she was dancing with him now. The pair swept by, Kennard tall and dark and serene, Rafella radiant, flushed, abandoned to pleasure, both of them regardless of the sombre, jealous eyes that watched them from the wall.

Mrs. Greaves, having twisted her ankle romping through a set of lancers, had now taken refuge on the dais for a precautionary rest; and she also watched the fairy figure floating round the room. Her neighbour on the red velvet settee happened to be the consort of a high official, a wise and benevolent lady, whose long experience of Indian life had only increased her natural kindness of heart and broadened her tolerant views.

"You know the Coventrys rather well, don't you, Mrs. Greaves?" she asked, as she followed the direction of the other woman's eyes. The question was not prompted by trivial curiosity, nor by any desire for ungenerous gossip, and of this Mrs. Greaves was fully aware, knowing her companion's disposition.

"I thought I knew Mrs. Coventry well," she said doubtfully, "but lately I've not felt quite sure. Can you believe that when she came out she considered it wrong to dress becomingly, or to do anything that might improve her appearance? And she thought we were all so fast and frivolous! She has altered so curiously."

"I am sorry for her, poor, pretty little person." The elder woman's placid face grew sad. "She is a typical example of the kind of girl who deteriorates rapidly in India; and then people at home, who won't try to understand, think India is to blame. She would have been just the same in England, or anywhere else, if she had been pitchforked into a different kind of life. If she doesn't come to grief, as I fear seems likely, she will probably go home and talk about her servants and her carriage and her men friends, and help to spread the false impression that out here all English women live like princesses and are nothing but brainless butterflies. It is such a mistake! She means no harm, I am sure, which makes it all the more regrettable."

"I also think she is far more to be pitied than blamed," agreed Mrs. Greaves. "She led such a narrow little life at home in a country vicarage, as far as I can gather from what she has told me at different times; and somehow it does seem to have unbalanced her to have a lady's maid, as she would call her ayah at first, and a smart dog-cart and big rooms, and plenty of society, and to discover that she was pretty and attractive. The worst of it is Captain Coventry doesn't understand the situation in the least, and makes no allowance."

"He ought not to leave her so much to look after herself. He appears to be always out shooting, or playing cricket or racquets or polo, when he isn't on duty. I suppose he's the wrong kind of husband for an undeveloped creature like that. She ought to have married a curate at home, or a small country squire; then she would probably have remained contented all her life, teaching in the Sunday school, and visiting the cottagers, and doing good according to her own ideas."

"You see," explained Mrs. Greaves, "at first Captain Coventry was only rather amused at the way many of her little scruples fizzled out, and treated her like a child—after all, in some ways she isn't much more—until she began to do things that most of us deprecate, though we know they are probably harmless enough. When she took up with this horrible man he got angry, and they had rows. You know, I dare say, how intolerant he is; he always thinks the worst of women. I have never really liked him, and I'm afraid, if it were not for Rafella's sake, I should feel rather pleased, in a way, that his selection had not turned out quite the paragon of propriety he expected."

"Can't you do anything? Can't you speak to her? I don't feel I know her sufficiently well to interfere."

"I did try, but it was hopeless. She seemed to think she was the only person with any principles in the station. She said I had an evil mind, that we all had evil minds, and she stuck to it that she was doing nothing wrong; and, literally speaking, I am sure she isn't; she's only being foolish. She declared that as long as her conscience was clear she did not see why she should give up her friendship with Mr. Kennard."

"I cannot abide that man! What on earth do some women see in him—or some men either, for that matter? It makes me so angry to hear them alluding to 'dear old Kennard.' No doubt he is clever—all barristers are; but I consider that no woman can be seen about with him and keep her reputation. I don't wonder Captain Coventry looks like a bear with a sore head. I hope he will soon put his foot down and stop the flirtation altogether."

"Yes, if he only does it the right way," said Mrs. Greaves doubtfully; and as the music ceased she observed, with apprehension, that Mr. Kennard and Mrs. Coventry were making for a screened-in, dimly lit veranda, and that Captain Coventry was following the couple with slow, determined steps.

"Oh!" she exclaimed involuntarily, below her breath, "I hope there isn't going to be a row!"

"My dear," the Commissioner's wife assured her, "Mr. Kennard will take care there is no row—in public, at any rate. That would not suit him at all."

"But Rafella is so silly, and Captain Coventry is so hard and vindictive. What will be the end of it?"

"If anyone goes to the wall, it will without question be the woman," said the other grimly; "that is what always happens in these deplorable cases."

Captain Coventry came upon his wife and her partner seated in an alcove. The pink glow from a paper lantern fell on the woman's fair head and delicate neck. She looked the picture of purity and innocence. The pair might have sat as models for Faust and Marguerite. Rafella glanced up quickly as her husband approached, walking slowly, evenly, along the veranda between the rows of sitting-out couples. She avoided his eyes as he came to a halt in front of her. Apparently Mr. Kennard did not see him.

"Are you ready to come home?" he asked in a cold, level voice.

Then she looked up in nervous appeal. "Oh, George, there are three more dances besides the extras on the programme!" She turned as though for sympathy and support to the man who sat silent at her side, toying with her fan. He only smiled inscrutably, and his eyes held the expression of one looking on at a comedy.

Captain Coventry stood rigid; his hands were clenched, his face hard and set.

"It is time for us to go home," he said, with a faint though unmistakable emphasis on the pronoun.

She moved a small, satin-shod foot impatiently. "Oh, do let us stay a little longer," she protested; "nobody is going yet."

"*We* are," said her husband.

"Why?" she demanded in desperate defiance. Then she looked frightened, and rose with reluctance from her seat.

For a moment she glanced from one man to the other, disconcerted because Mr. Kennard had said nothing, had not asserted his claim to the dances that still were his on her programme. Suddenly she felt helpless, deserted, indignant. Mr. Kennard must think she was not her own mistress, that she could not do as she chose, that she allowed herself to be treated like a child. It was insufferable! Why couldn't George trust her? He ought to be glad to see her receiving admiration and attention. It was odious of him to place her in such a false and unpleasant position. But while that hard, cruel look remained in his eyes she dared not defy him. She would have to obey like a slave at the moment, though she vowed to herself that she would demand an apology once they were alone.

She rose with an air of offended pride, and held out her hand for her fan. Kennard gave it to her with a bow, and a suppressed smile on his face that made Coventry long to knock him down. They bade each other formal good-nights, and Rafella stalked in the direction of the cloakroom, her head held high, her husband following her close.

On their way back to their bungalow there was silence between the Coventrys. They were driving in the cab of the country, a rough vehicle that resembled a palanquin on wheels, with venetian shutters instead of windows, and the noise it made would have rendered even the most amiable of conversations impossible. The air outside was warm and still, and the rattle of the wheels and the woodwork, and the clumsy harness, seemed intensified by the surrounding silence of the Indian night. The stuffy conveyance was filled with the scent of violets—lately Rafella had taken to scent, strong scent that clung and impregnated everything she wore. At her breast was a cluster of violets that had come from the pots in Mr. Kennard's veranda, and now, dying, the flowers gave out a stale fragrance. To the angry man at her side the concentrated perfume was atrocious. It seemed to be connected in some subtle way with the alteration in his wife's behaviour—to breathe of all that was false and worthless in a woman's heart. Bitterly he blamed the follies and temptations of Indian life, and her failure to withstand them. It did not occur to him that, with her limited intelligence, her inexperience of life, and her undeveloped outlook, things would have been the same in any quarter of the earth, given the scope and opportunity. He was a man who could not make allowances, who could perceive no point of view except his own; yet withal he was a straight and honourable English soldier, with high standards of right and wrong, and a deep sense of the sanctity of marriage. Such people are often incapable of distinguishing between mere foolishness and sin; they will argue that there are no degrees of infidelity, and that a false step necessarily implies complete downfall. Coventry had no sympathy with sexual temptation; in his sight, if a married woman permitted a man who was not her husband to make love to her, she was guilty of more than indiscretion.

His anger kept him silent as they entered their bungalow. He was afraid to trust himself to speak.

It was his wife who precipitated the storm; she turned up the lamp that was burning low on a table in the drawing-room, and threw her cloak on to a chair with a petulant movement. The atmosphere of the room was oppressive, yet Coventry had re-bolted the long glass door by which they had entered. Mosquitoes, disturbed by the light, flew with thin screamings around their heads.

For a moment they looked at each other. The man's eyes were cold and contemptuous, and the woman's sense of injury and injustice increased till she felt wellnigh desperate. To think that she should have been dragged home like a naughty little girl from a party, who must be sent to bed as a punishment, while everyone else was still dancing and enjoying the ball!—and Mr. Kennard would have found another partner whose husband was not a monster of unreasonable jealousy. Perhaps he would smile and shrug his shoulders, and cease now to send her violets every morning, and no longer single her out for special attention, or send her little notes asking what were her plans for the afternoon—or give her books with quotations inscribed by himself on the flyleaf: quotations conveying a harmless though flattering homage. In short, all the little inarticulate attentions that to the initiated are but the preliminaries to a game that need be no more than an emotional pastime, but may be fraught with peril to the flattered novitiate.

Instinctively her hand rested on a small, beautifully bound volume that had come this morning with the violets she wore, whose perfume stirred her senses even at this moment as it floated out into the room. On the title page was traced in Kennard's peculiar writing:

> *"A book of verses underneath the bough,*
> *A jug of wine, a loaf of bread, and* thou
> *Beside me, singing in the wilderness—*
> *Oh! wilderness were paradise enow."*

"Aren't you going to explain?" she demanded in a stifled voice. "You have made me the laughing-stock of the station. You have spoilt my evening. Do you expect me to submit without a word? I am not a child, let me tell you; I am capable of taking care of myself."

"Apparently that is just what you are not capable of doing," said Coventry. "Unless you promise me to behave decently in future, and unless you do so, I shall send you home to your father until my time is up in India."

A sudden remembrance of the shabby vicarage assailed her, and the dull little village, and the routine of housework, and economy; Sunday school, choir practice, parish duties, old people, the long dark winters, and the cold, and the rain, and the solitude. It chilled her spirit, and filled her with a sickening dread. Yet how could she bring herself to promise "to behave with decency," when, in her own opinion, she had done nothing reprehensible? Her "friendship" with Mr. Kennard was blameless on both sides. It might be true that he did not bear the best of characters; Mrs. Greaves had warned her, most officiously, of that, and had cited one or two so-called scandals in which he had been concerned, to all appearances, discreditably. But had he not told her himself, repeatedly, that it had all been the fault of the women, which she could quite believe, and that her influence on his life was the one good thing that had ever come his way? Had he not declared that for her sweet sake there should be no more "stories," that because of her he would be strong? Surely that was something to be proud of! Therefore, how could she turn and treat him as though he were a blackguard, and deny him the first incentive he had ever known to rectitude of life? Why, every Sunday lately he had gone to church at her behest, and he said he had given up gambling at the club, assured her that every night he read a chapter of the Bible she had lent him—a worn little volume that had been hers since childhood, with notes in the margins, and flowers pressed between the pages to mark the anniversaries of her life's rare events—her mother's death, her confirmation, her first communion, and her marriage.

"Well?" Her husband's voice cut sharply through her thoughts.

Now she gazed at him with large, distressed blue eyes.

"Oh, George, do try to understand! There is really nothing wrong. We are only friends, and he *needs* my friendship; it helps him, it does him good."

Rage and disgust almost choked him. "Bah!" he exclaimed furiously, "don't talk rot like that to me." He took a step forward, and seized her wrist. "Can you swear to me that the beast has never attempted to make love to you? Can you deny that he follows you about, and writes you notes, and gives you presents, and that you have never tried to stop him? The fellow is notorious, and only a man who was a fool or a blackguard would stand by and see his wife go to the devil with him or with anyone else."

She trembled, terrified, and her face became distorted with tears. "You are cruel and unjust," she sobbed. "I will not bear it."

He dropped her arm, and paced backwards and forwards among the furniture. Then he stopped by the table and picked up a book—the daintily bound little volume that had come for Rafella this morning. He looked at it with contempt.

"This is the kind of unwholesome rot he tries to poison your mind with." He opened the cover, and read the verse on the fly-leaf; next moment he flung the book to the farther end of the room.

"That is enough," he said. "Listen to me! If you don't promise me this instant never to speak to the man again, I'll—I'll kill you."

Coventry was beside himself with passion, for it seemed to him that his honour, his home, his name was besmirched. He felt humiliated, wronged; and the primitive sense of outraged possession had him in its grip. Nothing could ever be the same again between his wife and himself. It was all he could do not to strike her as she stood there, white, and fair, and weak, at his mercy, yet still with a frightened defiance in her childish blue eyes.

There followed a tense pause, as with set teeth he strove to master his passion, holding his clenched hands down on the table before him. . . And suddenly the silence outside was broken by the sound of wheels and the sharp trotting of a horse's hoofs that turned into the adjoining compound and ceased. Instinctively Rafella turned her head and listened. Mr. Kennard had come home from the ball. The knowledge that he was at hand gave her a feeling of partial security. That, together with indignation and resentment, kept her firm in her resolve not to be browbeaten into a promise that could only be an admission of guilt. She could not perceive that morally she had erred, though actually she was innocent of wrongdoing. It was precisely what her husband could not perceive either; to him there was little difference.

"Are you going to promise?" he asked, with menace in his voice.

She put up her hands as though to shield herself from violence.

"Are you going to promise?" he said again, and moved a little nearer.

Then her courage failed her. She was afraid of George, afraid of the look on his face that reminded her of a savage animal—afraid of his threats, and his voice, and his presence. She turned and ran to the door that had been bolted by him as they entered. He followed her. She screamed, stretching her white arms up to the bolt, dragging it down.

Next moment she was outside, running in silent terror towards the house in the next compound. The lightly clad figure sped like a ghost through the dim light of the coming dawn, and stumbled through the gap in the low mud boundary, leaving George Coventry standing on the threshold of his house as though he had been turned to stone.

Motionless he stood; then he laughed like a drunken man, and reeled back into the room that smelt of matting and lamp-oil and—violets.

THE DISAPPEARANCE OF MR. KENNARD AND Mrs. Coventry came as a veritable bombshell to the station. Nobody knew exactly what had happened; there were so many different stories. Hitherto people had noticed and talked, some with jealous interest, others more or less good-naturedly, a few with real regret, but none with any expectation of a serious scandal; for domestic disaster is rare in India, in spite of popular delusion to the contrary. And when it occurs, partly because of its rarity, partly because in any community so intimate as one class of the same nationality in exile, such an occurrence goes sharply home, and creates a sensation at once so painful and exciting that it is not quickly forgotten.

It was said that Mrs. Coventry had deliberately left her husband after a terrible scene; another version was that she had confessed on the night of the bachelors' ball to conduct such as had left Captain Coventry no alternative but to allow her to go; again that he had turned her out, and she had sought refuge in Mr. Kennard's bungalow. Someone had seen the runaway couple leaving next day by the mail train for Bombay. The more charitable maintained that the injured husband had been chiefly to blame; he had made a mountain out of a molehill, would listen to no explanation, nor give the benefit of any doubt, driving his wife to the ruinous step she had taken.

All that remained evident was that Mrs. Coventry and Mr. Kennard were no longer seen in the station, and that for a short space of time Captain Coventry continued to perform his regimental duties, to play polo and racquets and cricket, in taciturn silence. His bearing inhibited questions, or mention to him of what had occurred; no one dared to intrude on his secret, and his reticence was respected. A little later he took leave on urgent private affairs and went home; and in due time an undefended divorce case, with Mr. Kennard as co-respondent, was reported without detail in the papers.

Mr. Kennard was eventually heard of in another Province, where, from all accounts, he was as popular as ever with a certain section of society always to be found anywhere, people who are attracted by good dinners and a display of wealth and an apparently superior knowledge of the world, who are content to ask no questions—which they call minding their own business.

Gossip subsided with the fluctuation of the European population of a large Indian station, where the military portion come and go, and civil officials are constantly transferred. Captain Coventry did not come back; he exchanged into the home battalion of his regiment. There came echoes and whispers that little Mrs. Coventry had returned to India after the decree had been made absolute, under the confiding impression that Mr. Kennard would make her his wife. But some declared that, of course, he was not such a fool; others that he had been blackguard enough to refuse to marry her; and what became of her nobody knew, and very few cared; for, after all, it was no one's immediate affair.

Chapter 7

TRIXIE

It was sixteen years since the night of the ball in India when Mrs. Greaves had twisted her ankle, and had sat on the dais with the wife of a senior civilian discussing the unfortunate domestic affairs of Captain and Mrs. Coventry.

Now Mrs. Greaves's husband was a retired colonel, and they were living comfortably, if dully, within their means in a convenient suburb of London, engrossed in the careers of their boys, content with their surroundings, with their well-built villa, their well-trained maids, their patch of garden and their neighbours—mostly staunch old Indian friends.

Until lately Mrs. Munro, now for years a widow, had been one of these neighbours, living quietly with Trixie her daughter at the end of the Greaves's road in a little house called "Almorah." Hereabouts many of the houses bore names reminiscent of India—rather pathetic links with a past that some of the occupants frequently glorified into "happier days," forgetting as frequently how they had pined for an English home while living in exile. More or less unconsciously the little colony of "old Indians" preserved among themselves various propensities acquired during their service abroad. For example, they bought each others' furniture, borrowed and loaned belongings with ready good nature, paid informal visits chiefly in the mornings, quarrelled sometimes about nothing, and were inclined to be exclusive outside their own circle.

They were all very happy and comfortable in spite of past glories, whether real or imagined, and when Trixie Munro grew up and clamoured for change, her godmother, Marion Greaves ("Gommie," as Trixie had called her ever since she could talk), urged Ellen Munro to let well alone and stay where she was—to pay no attention to Trixie's ridiculous hankerings after a London flat.

"You can't afford the move, my dear," she had said with truth, "and the sooner Trixie learns that other things matter besides her own whims the better." Trixie and Gommie were more often at war than on terms of peace.

However, persuasions and warnings failed, the obstacle being that the mother's whole life was bound up in the child, and for Trixie to be disappointed meant double distress for Mrs. Munro. Therefore the removal from "Almorah" to the flat in West Kensington, which was all Mrs. Munro could achieve on her income, had been accomplished in direct opposition to Mrs. Greaves's concerned and strenuous advice.

Now, on a wet afternoon in January Mrs. Greaves was starting from her suburban home to have tea in "Mulberry Mansions, West Kensington, W.," with Ellen Munro. Though her once crisp chestnut hair was faded and grey, and her sharp little face had lost its freshness and its freckles—no longer could she claim to be called "The Plover's Egg"—she had kept her health and her trimness of figure, and had lost none of her practical, vigorous grip on existence.

She selected an umbrella—not her best—from the stand in the hall, and opened the front door. A cold, wet wind blew into her face; the outlook was not encouraging, and the walk to the station would hardly be pleasant in such horrible weather. But with her usual determination she closed the door firmly behind her, giving it a pull to make sure it was shut, and set off in the wind and the rain undaunted. She trudged down the hill, traversed a long stretch of road bounded chiefly by boards that advertised plots of "desirable" land for building, and arrived at the tram-riddled town. On the way to the station, she entered a flower shop and purchased a large bunch of violets.

When she emerged from the underground railway station into the muddy London street, she had to wrestle with the second-best umbrella that endeavoured to turn inside out. It was a ten minutes' walk to the Munros' little flat, and that she was carrying the large bunch of violets in a paper cone added to her difficulties in the wind and the rain; but she was wearing an old coat and skirt, and she felt it would be an unnecessary extravagance to take a cab. Ellen Munro would provide shoes and stockings while her own were being dried in the kitchen. She knew that Ellen was at home only to herself on the periodical occasions when she came up from the suburb for tea and a talk over old times.

The cold and the wet and the gloom of this January day had not deterred her from the expedition, for Ellen Munro had written to say she had an important communication to impart to her old friend, and, as a human being as well as an old friend, Marion Greaves was agog to know the news. She speculated as to what it could possibly be as she paddled along the slippery pavement; in all probability it was something connected with Trixie, and she wondered what the tiresome girl had been doing now. Seeing that Trixie was her goddaughter, Mrs. Greaves felt she was entitled to interfere when the child behaved more outrageously than usual. She had always considered that Ellen Munro was not sufficiently strict with the girl, allowing Trixie to be capricious and extravagant and to do just as she chose! The result some day must certainly be disastrous. What else could be expected when the mother was so weak and indulgent, and the daughter so selfish and irresponsible? The modern girl seemed to be a terrible problem, and Mrs. Greaves felt glad she had only to think of two sons, who were shaping well and would soon be supporting themselves.

She was thankful, presently, to find herself in the warm, though shabby, little drawing-room that was pathetically embellished with Indian relics—embroideries that were dulled with the London atmosphere, bits of brass and Cashmere silverwork that the cook-general had no time to clean, intricate carvings of scented wood, warped and dusty. She laid her offering of violets on a chair, where it lay neglected in the little bustle of greeting and the shedding of her wet shoes. She had bought the flowers for Ellen, who had plenty of vases, though she could seldom fill them, she could not afford niceties; every extra penny was needed for Trixie, so that Trixie need not go ill-dressed among her young friends—friends of whom Mrs. Munro inwardly disapproved, yet could not refuse to acknowledge without unpleasantness with Trixie. Silly, irresponsible boys and girls, who practically ignored Mrs. Munro when they came to the flat, and made up parties with Trixie for second-rate subscription dances, afternoons and evenings at skating rinks, tango teas, river picnics, and so on. Trixie's mother strove to give her daughter adequate pocket-money, so that taxi fares, gloves, sweets, cigarettes should not become too acceptable from young men friends.

Soon the visitor's feet were dry and warm, the cook-general had at last ceased to come in and out of the room, and the tea-kettle was boiling.

"Now," said Mrs. Greaves, "what is it?"

"Trixie is going to be married." Trixie's mother did not look at her old friend as she spoke. She gazed into the fire, and there was a certain defensiveness in her voice.

"Good gracious, my dear Ellen, why didn't you tell me in your letter?"

"You are the first person I have told," said Mrs. Munro evasively.

"Well, are you pleased? Who is he? Has he any money?"

"I suppose I am pleased, but he is so much older than Trixie." There was a pause.

"Really, Ellen, considering we have known each other since we were girls, I think you might be a little more anxious to tell me all about it."

"I know I must seem horrid, but it has been worrying me rather, and I hardly know yet what to feel or say."

"At any rate, tell me the man's name?" Mrs. Greaves regarded the worn, white face of her friend with impatient anxiety. Incidentally, she wished Ellen would leave off her mourning; she had been a widow for so many years, and black had never suited her.

"It is Colonel Coventry," said Ellen, with an effort.

"Coventry? Surely not the man we knew in India—in the Barchesters?"

Mrs. Munro nodded, and there was silence between the two women, who were both thinking of Trixie, aged nineteen, pretty, pleasure-loving, wilful, as the wife of a man nearly thirty years her senior; a man, moreover, who had been noted for his intolerance of feminine frailty, for his almost puritanical views where the conduct of women was concerned. How could such a marriage prove a success on either side?

"But, Ellen——" began Mrs. Greaves, and hesitated. Then she added quickly: "Does Trixie know that he was married before, and that he divorced his wife?"

"Yes; she doesn't seem to mind. She says it was all such a long time ago. You know what Trixie is when she has made up her mind and wants to do a thing."

"I know what girls are nowadays, and Trixie in particular," said Mrs. Greaves rather tartly. "I suppose Colonel Coventry's first marriage must seem prehistoric to her, but sixteen years to us is not so long ago. At any rate, let us hope it will steady her to be married to a man old enough to be her father."

Mrs. Munro's soft eyes filled with tears. She said in plaintive protest: "You are always so hard on Trixie, Marion. There is no real harm in the child. She only likes to enjoy herself in her own way."

"She will not be permitted to enjoy herself in her own way as Mrs. Coventry, unless he has altered very much since I knew him. It will have to be his way or nothing. Ellen, I should not like to see a girl of mine, however well balanced, married to that man. I believe him to be hard and unsympathetic. Remember how he behaved to his first wife, even as a comparatively young man. The whole station blamed him."

"I was at home that year; it was after I took Trixie home; but I remember hearing about the case. Surely Mrs. Coventry only got what she deserved? How could he have done anything but divorce her when he found out what she was?"

"My dear, I always doubted if there was anything to find out beyond extreme foolishness, though appearances were certainly against her. I knew her fairly well, and I never for one moment thought she had been really bad. George Coventry was one of those men who are ready to believe the worst about women, and who pose as saints themselves. Does Trixie profess to be in love with him, may I ask?"

"She seems happy. He's very good-looking, and she admires him." Mrs. Munro spoke helplessly. Then she reached behind her and took from a small table a silver-framed photograph of a man in uniform—just the head and shoulders—a stern, handsome face, with close-cropped grey hair and grave, keen eyes.

Mrs. Greaves regarded it intently. "He has grown better-looking with age," she remarked. "He looks like an elderly hero in a play. I dare say he might take a young girl's fancy." As she handed the photograph back to Ellen Munro she espied another photograph on the table, that of a young man, cheerful, impudent, boyish.

"What will Guy say when he hears of Trixie's engagement, I wonder?"

"What should he say? There was nothing between him and Trixie, and never could have been. They both knew that quite well."

"All the same, it is fortunate, perhaps, that she is not going to India."

"But she *is* going to India," said Mrs. Munro desperately. "George takes up command of that battalion next month, and he wants Trixie to be ready to go with him. She is quite willing."

"Ah!" exclaimed Mrs. Greaves significantly; and Trixie's mother sat silent, in rueful understanding.

Guy Greaves, Colonel Greaves's nephew, was a subaltern in the battalion of the Barchesters now serving in India, and it was through him, indirectly, that Trixie had met the man she had promised to marry. Some people might have imagined that she was more likely to marry the subaltern than the colonel, until that youth left England, glum and miserable; and there was one young man the less to go with Trixie and her friends to teas and dances and theatres—outings he could ill afford, "broke," as he had always declared himself, "to the world."

Presently Mrs. Munro said: "What could I do, except refuse my consent until Trixie was of age? Of course, I had to consent. I felt I had no right to raise objections that could only be indefinite. As you know, we have nothing but our pensions, and it is a galling life to a girl of Trixie's temperament. Colonel Coventry has private means, and his character is unimpeachable. There are no drawbacks beyond his age and his sad story."

Mrs. Munro's voice trembled; she was almost at the end of her endurance, and she began to cry in the silent, helpless manner peculiar to women of her down-trodden type. All her life she had been sacrificed to somebody; first to her brother, who had been considered in every way before herself; then to her husband's mother and sisters, since the greater part of Mr. Munro's pay had gone home towards their support, and he had died before he could save anything for his wife and child; and then to Trixie, who had always had what she wanted as far as the widow's slender means would permit, and of late had been "such a handful," to quote Mrs. Greaves and various other of the mother's old friends.

The heart of Marion Greaves smote her. She had a genuine affection for Ellen Munro—the affection that is born of custom and propinquity. They had known each other for so many years, and had been through so much together, and having no daughter of her own Marion was deeply, if tiresomely, interested in Ellen's only girl. As Trixie's godmother she felt doubly entitled to speak her mind on the subject of Trixie's faults. She never hesitated to tell the girl she was vain and selfish and rebellious; that, though it might be true she dusted the drawing-room and darned her own stockings, she ought also to darn her mother's, and help in the kitchen and bedrooms as well, not to speak of making some sort of attempt to keep down current expenses, instead of straining her mother's income to breaking point with her gaieties and her clothes.

Unknown to Trixie, Mrs. Greaves had more than once helped Ellen through a difficulty with a so-called loan, which was afterwards transformed into a Christmas or a birthday present, despite Mrs. Munro's grateful protests; and if, in return, Marion claimed the right to say what she thought, Mrs. Munro felt that the least she could do was to submit amiably to the raps of home truths. Trixie, however, was not so accommodating, and when Mrs. Greaves was expected to tea she generally contrived to have a pressing engagement elsewhere. Even the miserable weather to-day had not inclined her to listen to her mother's supplications that she should stay at home for once to see "Gommie."

"I have some regard for my nose," she had declared, "and I should certainly get it bitten off altogether if I gave Gommie the chance this afternoon."

Now, while Ellen Munro wept, Marion Greaves put more coal on the fire and stirred up a cheerful blaze. She also pulled down the blinds and drew the curtains.

"There," she said, "that's better. Have some more tea, Ellen," she added remorsefully, "and don't mind what I say. I know as well as you do that there's no real harm in the child. It's only a question if George Coventry will realise it when she is his wife, and make allowances for her youth and high spirits. If he manages her judiciously, I don't doubt that she will respond, for I must own that, with all her faults, the child has an honest nature. After all, you have done what seems to you best, and nobody can do more. They must take their chance of understanding each other. Only you ought to give Trixie a *good* talking to before she goes out to India." Mrs. Greaves felt torn between sympathy for Ellen and apprehension for Trixie's future. "Now, what about the trousseau? Of course, she gets a sum down for that from the fund, which is a comfort, and I will give her a cheque to get what she likes as my wedding present."

Mrs. Munro's affectionate expressions of gratitude were muffled by her pocket handkerchief, but she soon allowed herself to be drawn into an interesting discussion concerning Trixie's outfit for India, though both ladies were well aware that they were not likely to be allowed much say in the matter.

Covertly Mrs. Greaves glanced at the clock. If she left at once she would be home in good time for dinner; if she stayed a little longer she would miss the next train, but she might see Trixie. Mrs. Munro was oblivious of the time; she was looking happier, more alive, and she described the engagement ring which George had brought in his pocket yesterday. Such lovely diamonds; and he was going to give Trixie a pendant, and all sorts of other delightful things.

Mrs. Greaves very nearly said: "I wonder what became of his presents to the first Mrs. Coventry?" but she refrained, and the next moment the door was opened and Trixie came in, followed by Colonel Coventry.

Even "Gommie" was struck silent by the girl's beauty. She looked so vivid, so radiant, fresh from the cold and the wet outside, though her hat was crammed on to her neck, which raised the ire of Mrs. Greaves.

"Such shocking style!" she commented inwardly. Then she looked beyond Trixie to the man who was to be the girl's husband, and found herself forced to admit that, despite the difference in their ages, they made a handsome and unusual pair. Colonel Coventry was obviously devoted, and Trixie looked elated. She introduced "George" to "Gommie" with scarcely concealed pride and triumph.

A shadow crossed the man's face when Mrs. Greaves claimed him as an old acquaintance.

"I remember you very well," she said, "years ago in India. You have not been back there since those days, have you?"

"No," he answered shortly.

Mrs. Munro fluttered to the rescue. "Mrs. Greaves's nephew, Guy Greaves, is in your regiment, you know, George. It was through him, somehow, that you came across Trixie, wasn't it?"

"I believe I owe him that debt," he said, smiling; "and no doubt I shall be expected to remember it when he wants leave out of his turn."

They all laughed rather artificially, and Mrs. Greaves remarked how curious it was that most people who had been in India found themselves linked up in some way or another.

"Your future mother-in-law and I are such very old friends, and now you are going to marry my goddaughter, and there is Guy in your regiment. It all goes round in a circle."

Then she looked at the clock. "Well, I must be going, or I shall miss my train. Trixie, my dear, I hope you will be very happy and that you will try to be a good wife."

"Oh, Gommie, don't be so depressing. Do say for a change that you hope George will make a good husband. That is much more to the point. How could I be happy if he should turn out to be a tyrant, and beat and ill-use me? You know, they say it doesn't matter who you marry, because you are sure to find out afterwards that you have married somebody else."

Mrs. Greaves, regarding her with godmotherly affection, as well as with disapproval, thought of the night at the railway station in India, such years ago, when Trixie had laughed and chattered and danced up and down at the window of the compartment, grabbing her toy, while her parents were breaking their hearts in farewell. Then she was only a baby and could not be blamed for her callousness; yet now at nineteen she seemed almost as heartless!

"I am sure," said Mrs. Greaves dryly, "that it will be your own fault if he does beat you, and that you will richly deserve it."

"Help!" cried Trixie.

Mrs. Greaves addressed herself to Mrs. Munro. "Now, Ellen, may I go into the kitchen and put on my own shoes and stockings? They must have been dry long ago. I only trust your maid has not allowed them to scorch."

The two ladies left the room, and Trixie looked at herself appreciatively in the mirror over the mantelpiece and hummed a gay tune.

"Gommie is a cat," she said carelessly. "She thinks I am a sort of she-devil, and I am sure she was longing to tell you dreadful things about my frivolity, and want of heart, and my general wickedness."

There was no response, and she turned to see George Coventry regarding her with serious eyes.

"Perhaps she would also tell you that I was hard, and cold, and intolerant," he said brusquely.

"Well, if you are I shall come home again, and enjoy myself as a grass widow," she laughed.

"Trixie!" he protested; and her youth, her sweetness, her bright eyes overcame him, rendered him weak and fatuous. He caught her in his arms and kissed her passionately; she submitted with a sort of gracious triumph. He released her reluctantly. "I wonder," he said, "if I am doing wrong in taking you? My life is half over, yours is only just beginning. You have no experience, and mine has been a hard one. Do you know, child, that I swore I would never believe in a woman again? And then you came and conquered, and made me feel I had everything left to live for if you would be my wife. Trixie"—his voice held an agony of doubt—"you won't fail me? You will keep alive my new-found faith? You will be a true and loving wife?"

She quailed a little at his vehemence, as though she had a sudden glimpse of something far more deep and serious than had yet come within her knowledge.

"I will try," she faltered, half-frightened. Then her gay spirit reasserted itself. "But you are not going to expect me to stay at home and mend your socks and sew on your buttons the *whole* time, are you? I may go to dances, and join in theatricals, and ride, and play tennis, and enjoy myself now and then, mayn't I?" She looked at him mischievously.

He sighed rather hopelessly. "I'm too old for you, Trixie. I don't dance, and I can't act, though I certainly can ride and play tennis. I must confess I prefer staying at home to going out in the evening, though it will be a different matter now, altogether, going out with you."

"Oh, you shan't be dragged forth when you don't want to go," she said, with mock encouragement. "Guy Greaves can always take me if you don't feel inclined to turn out. I've known Guy since we were both children. He's a dear boy, and he does dance so well. He had tango lessons when he was at home last summer, and he picked it up at once."

George Coventry's face darkened. "No other man will take you out while *I* am your husband!" he said violently.

"Oh, George, are you going to be jealous?" she cried in genuine consternation.

"I shall not be jealous unless you give me cause," he said heatedly. "But I have no intention of playing the rôle of the complaisant husband, if that is what you mean."

"Oh, don't look so horrid and ogreish. If you can't trust me, you had better say so at once. If you imagine I am capable of doing anything that isn't cricket, we'd better agree to end our engagement. But I thought"— her voice broke and tears rose in her eyes—"I thought you really cared for me, and wanted me to be your wife and not your slave." She turned from him to conceal her tearful annoyance and agitation.

Instantly he was all remorse and repentance. "What a brute I am! Trixie, darling, do try to understand. It's only because I love you so deeply, so truly, that I can't bear to think of your having even a pleasure that I can't share with you. I want all of you, Trixie, all your confidence and your thoughts, and your moods and your companionship. My life would be impossible now without you."

She responded generously. "I know you didn't mean to be beastly," she said, smiling her forgiveness at him. "You must take me as I am or leave me. And don't forget that I am taking you as you are, too, cross old patch." She gave him a flippant little kiss on his chin.

Then, with an exclamation of surprise and pleasure, she noticed the paper cone filled with violets that had been left on a chair and forgotten by her mother and Mrs. Greaves in the engrossment of their converse.

"Oh, delicious things!" She took them up and smelt them, then held them out to Colonel Coventry. "How sweet they are! Don't you love violets? Do violets grow in India, George?"

He recoiled from the fragrance as though it were some poisonous odour.

"I can't endure them," he said shortly.

MEANWHILE, MRS. GREAVES WAS ON HER way, in the rain and the wind, to the station. "If history doesn't repeat itself," she was reflecting in anxious forebodement, "I shall be very thankful, but very much surprised."

When she got home she informed her husband that Ellen Munro was even a greater fool than she had always believed her to be.

"What has she been doing now?" he inquired, without particular interest.

"She has allowed Trixie to get engaged to that Coventry man we knew a hundred years ago in India. He is old enough to be her father, and he divorced his wife for nothing, and never bothered himself afterwards as to what became of her when the other man didn't marry her."

"Coventry? But he wasn't at all a bad sort of fellow!" said Colonel Greaves. "As straight as they make 'em, and such a good shot, if that is the man you mean. I remember his wife. Now *she* was a fool, if you like; he was far too good for her."

"You men always stick up for each other," protested his wife. "No doubt you are as ready to praise that horrible man who ruined poor Mrs. Coventry's life. I can't remember his name at this moment."

Colonel Greaves wisely made no reply.

Chapter 8

INDIA

U p country in India spring is a period of conflicting impressions. The sharp—sometimes almost too sharp—bite of the cold season has yielded to a warm and languorous atmosphere, perfumed powerfully with mango blossom; dew still beads the grass at dawn; English flowers luxuriate, impelled to rarer bloom and fragrance. There comes a sense of ease and peace, and scented calm, that would be blissful but for the lurking knowledge that the sun is only just withholding the full fierceness of his power—giving "quarter," as it were—till preparations are complete to resist the trials of the true hot weather. Fans and punkahs must be fixed and hung, mosquito curtains washed and mended, screens of sweet kus-kus root made ready for the doorways, supplies of captive quail and teal laid in to tempt the jaded palate, when all day long the hot west wind would scorch and shrivel everything outside the darkened houses, and the temperature might stand as high at midnight as at noon.

At Patalpur the winter gaieties were over, and the bustle of departure to the hills had just begun. A feeling of temporary leisure pervaded the English quarter of the station, and Trixie Coventry could enjoy the pleasant interval the more because the drawbacks of the coming months were yet unknown to her. India was perfect. How she loved the sun, the space, the colour, the friendliness, and the novelty of her surroundings! Since her arrival she had revelled in a whirl of popularity; no one's party was complete without pretty Mrs. Coventry; her beauty, her high spirits, and the fact of her youth, contrasted with her position as a colonel's wife, made her exceptionally interesting. One or two "croakers" prophesied that it would surely turn her head, but the majority could not pay her too much attention.

Colonel Coventry bore it all with a fairly tolerant spirit. His work had been heavy, his leisure filled with unavoidable engagements that he recognised were multiplied tenfold because of his wife's perfections. He attended dinners, dances, at homes, but all the while he was covertly impatient for the lull to come, when he and Trixie might be more alone together, when she would settle down, of course, to months of domestic routine. With a certain relief he had observed that, so far, Trixie had given little time to the renewal of her boy-and-girl friendship with Guy Greaves, who seemed to have no special footing in her favour; and, indeed, Colonel Coventry found nothing to complain of in his wife's attitude towards any of her numerous admirers. She was indiscriminately gracious to them all, riding with one and the other, dancing with each in turn, laughing, chaffing, accepting their notes and offerings and adoration with a gay indifference that was unquestionably beyond criticism or gossip.

But now that his duties were slackening, now that he had more leisure to devote to his young wife, Colonel Coventry began to notice that he seldom had first claim on her companionship. She was so frequently engaged for rides, and for sets of tennis that she declared had "been made up ages ago, and could not possibly be chucked." And gradually Guy Greaves seemed to be more often her partner, and to be under promise to escort her on so many riding expeditions. To Colonel Coventry the young man now appeared to haunt the veranda, to be always either calling for Mrs. Coventry, or to have "just brought her back" from something. Inevitably, dissatisfaction began to creep into the husband's heart. He was not exactly jealous—that, he told himself, would be absurd. Trixie was so frank and open, and so clearly unconscious that she was doing anything to which anyone could take exception. Greaves was a mere boy, and, moreover, one of his own subalterns; and these facts deterred George Coventry from voicing his disapproval quite so soon as otherwise he might have done.

This evening he stood in the veranda of his bungalow waiting for Trixie to come home. Some regimental complication had called him away unexpectedly after luncheon, and he had forgotten to inquire before he started as to her plans for the afternoon. Therefore he had hurried back, intending to suggest a ride, but the bearer informed him she had already gone out with "Grivsahib." They had driven away in the sahib's dog-cart half an hour ago. Coventry, in his annoyance, imagined that the man's eyes held a veiled insolence, and the little rasp of irritation that had worried him of late increased now to definite displeasure with his wife. He went off to play racquets violently; then, calm and more controlled, he had returned, rather late, only to find that Trixie had not yet come back. His anger rose again, but when he had changed for dinner fear also beset him lest some harm had come to her, and it urged him out to the veranda.

Darkness, that in the East drops like a curtain, shrouded the compound; fireflies were sparkling in the trees, there was a smell of hot dust and tired blossoms in the warm, still air that seemed to hold no sound. He waited, anxious, angry, on the steps, listening intently for the roll of wheels and the beat of a pony's hoofs on the hard road. Once or twice he thought he heard the sounds he expected, but they died away without coming nearer, if they had really been audible at all; and then, as he waited and listened, there rose sharply, cruelly, in his mind the memory of another night in India, many years ago, when, from another bungalow, in another station, he had heard the rattle of a dog-cart driving swiftly into the adjoining compound. He became conscious of the scent of violets. In desperate resentment he moved forward to try and free himself from this spell of hideous recollection, and as he moved his foot struck against a flower-pot. He realised then that it was a pot of violets, and viciously he kicked it over the plinth of the veranda, and heard it smash to pieces as it fell.

The next moment Trixie and young Greaves drove in at the compound gate, laughing, and Trixie called out as the trap drew up before the steps: "Did you think we were lost, George?" She sprang lightly to the ground before he could descend to help her. "We *are* late, but we've had a lovely time. Won't you come in, Guy, and have a drink?"

"Not to-night, thanks." Then the boyish voice was raised in respectful apology: "So sorry, sir, but we couldn't help it. Mrs. Coventry will explain."

Trixie stood by her husband's side as the dog-cart turned to leave the compound, and she called after the retreating vehicle: "Don't forget the first time there's a moon!" And an answering shout came back: "All right! Good-night!"

She laid her hand on Coventry's arm. "You haven't been fidgeting, have you, George?"

There was no answer. He stood rigid, unresponsive.

"What's the matter? Are you cross?"

"I thought something must have happened to you," he said stiffly.

"Why, what could have happened? I was quite safe with Guy."

"Mr. Greaves," he corrected.

She laughed. "What nonsense! I've always called him Guy. Why should I begin 'mister-ing' him now? Come along in; I'm so hungry." She chattered on happily. "We went on the river and rowed for miles. It was simply lovely. We saw crocodiles, and a funeral pyre on the bank, with the relations all standing round and the smoke curling up. And then we landed and got into a grove full of tombstones. Guy said he believed it was an old Mohammedan burying-ground. So funny, with Hindu corpses being burnt just below it. What a mixed-up place India seems to be!"

"What made you so late?" he asked, following her into the drawing-room, that was bright and pretty with lamplight and wedding presents and chintz-covered chairs, though it felt a little close and airless.

"Poof!" said Trixie. "How hot it is in the house! Do let us have dinner out of doors."

"We should be smothered with insects," he objected. "We can't dine outside without lamps when there's no moon."

"Directly there's a moon," said Trixie, "I'm going to ride out with Guy to that wood and sit on a tombstone and look at the river. And then we will tango—tango in and out among the trees."

She danced a few steps, singing, down the middle of the room. She looked so gay, so full of life and health, so pretty in her white silk blouse cut open at the neck, and her short drill skirt, and a Panama hat slouched over her forehead, that Coventry's anger melted to a sad regret. He had never felt quite sure of her, never certain that she cared for him; indeed, deep in his heart he knew that Trixie was yet ignorant of love; and he was tortured with the half-acknowledged dread that out of some thoughtless flirtation with another man there might arise a primal passion that would wreck his life again and hers. To-night the memory of Rafella, and the dreadful moment of their parting, was so uncannily insistent that he felt as though he stood on the brink of another crisis—one that would be infinitely worse for him. He loved Trixie as he had never loved his former wife—a mature, strong love that held far less of self, combining almost a paternal feeling with the deep devotion of a husband. And now it was poisoned with a helpless, jealous sense of danger that he could not combat. It came between him and his desire to behave wisely, warily, with tact towards her. His innate horror of gossip and scandal, his latent distrust of her friendship with young Greaves, added to the lingering influence of his alarm that some accident had befallen her to keep him out so late, held him harping on the question that she had not answered.

"You haven't told me why you were so late," he said.

"Oh, George, how you do bother! I don't know, except that I suppose we forgot the time, and then, driving home through the bazaar, we got into a sort of block—a native procession, a wedding, or a festival of some kind. There was a tremendous crowd and such a noise—tom-toms and horns and torches. We were delayed, I should think, for quite ten minutes, drawn up at the side of the street while it passed. Guy got so impatient, and wanted to barge through the middle of it, but, of course, I wouldn't let him. We should have knocked down dozens of people. And, besides, I was awfully interested and amused. I didn't want to go on. It never struck me that you might be anxious."

She ran into her room to dress for dinner, and he could hear her singing softly as she moved about. He resolved to say no more about her staying out so late to-night alone with young Greaves. If it happened again he would put down his foot once and for all. Meanwhile, he would drop a hint to the boy that his behaviour towards Mrs. Coventry should be rather more circumspect; and as to the moonlight expedition that Trixie seemed to contemplate, it would be time enough to deal with that if she talked of such a senseless prank again. Probably she would forget all about it.

He made every effort during dinner to be amiable and entertaining, to avoid any subject that might lead to disagreement, and Trixie responded in her happiest mood. Afterwards they sat outside in the veranda, lazing in their long cane chairs, talking little, quietly content, until suddenly, from the warm darkness of the compound, there came a harsh and piercing cry that rose to an excruciating pitch, then, note by note, sank back once more to silence.

"Oh! what was that?" she asked, startled.

But it was nothing more alarming than the trial song of India's cuckoo, the bird that is no harbinger of hope and life and all the joys of spring, as is his Western cousin, but the token of a time of stress and strain and trial only to be realised by those who have endured it.

"A brain-fever bird," he told her. "If I can see the beggar to-morrow I'll shoot him."

They listened as the sound rose and fell again, this time farther off.

"India rather frightens me," said Trixie, "and yet I get fits of fascination that make me feel as if the country had bewitched me. It all seems so old and so cruel, and yet so alluring. I felt the spell of it this evening on the river, and still more strongly when we were waiting in the bazaar for the procession to pass. That big city, full of people we really know nothing about, with all sorts of weird things happening in it that we never hear of. *I* think the bazaar is quite wonderful, but Guy Greaves said the smell of it was all that affected him, and his one idea was to get out of it."

"The young fool had no business to take you through the bazaar at all!" said Coventry, with suppressed irritation.

Disapproval invariably spurred Trixie to truculence. "It was the shortest way," she retorted with spirit, "and we were late as it was. How were we to know that we should be delayed by a procession?"

Coventry did not reply. He had no desire to embark on further argument with Trixie.

"I suppose," she went on idly, "there are no end of extraordinary stories buried away all over India. Do you think it is true that lots of white women were carried off in the Mutiny and were never seen again, or only heard of by accident?"

"I don't know," he said, with curt reluctance to discuss such a subject. "One hears all sorts of things."

One thing had been mentioned in his hearing only this afternoon, on the racquet court, that had filled him with disgust and horror—a whisper, a rumour, that a woman, an Englishwoman, was living in a certain quarter of the bazaar. The thought sickened him. Pah! it was atrocious, if true. It recurred to him unpleasantly, increasing his annoyance that his wife should have been exposed to the gaze of a crowd of excited natives in company with a man who was not her husband. In his opinion, the less Englishwomen were observed of Orientals the better. His determination strengthened that in future Trixie should have no escort but himself.

He found it easy to carry out his intention for the time being. Young Greaves was laid low with an attack of malaria, and afterwards he took a month's leave to join a rich globe-trotting relative on a little tour through native states. Trixie seemed quite content to ride with her husband and to have him for her partner on the tennis court. He rode extremely well and looked his best on horseback, and there were few couples who could hope to beat the Coventrys at tennis when they played together. Just then a small and select tournament was in progress, and Trixie held high hopes that she and George would win it. She coveted the prize—a handsome silver chain bag for the lady; and she meant to annex the cigarette-case as well that was to reward the victorious male partner. And George weakly promised she should have it if they won, though he disapproved entirely of women smoking, and hated to see Trixie with a cigarette between her red lips. All the same, it was a spectacle that had to be endured, for nothing he could say had yet persuaded Trixie to eschew the habit. Dances were in abeyance for the next few months, but there were little friendly dinners, and it was altogether a pleasant and congenial period, though daily the heat grew and brain-fever birds multiplied in the compounds, and people went out later in the afternoons and earlier in the mornings.

Chapter 9

DOUBT

Probably Coventry was happier just now than he had yet been during his lifetime. He had always known, he assured himself, that, once the first excitement of her new existence had subsided, Trixie would settle down; that it could only be a matter of time for her to realise the responsibilities of a married woman's life; which self-assurance was not exactly genuine. But when doubt has safely turned to confidence, many of us are apt to forget that doubt has ever troubled us at all. However, at last Trixie seemed to have entered upon a stage of domesticity, just as whole-heartedly as she had thrown herself at first into gaieties and social distractions. She became wildly enthusiastic over her housekeeping, and tried her own and her husband's digestions severely by her daring experiments in cookery. She started a farmyard, and was triumphant concerning eggs and poultry, while George was driven silently distracted by the piercing and persistent clack of guinea-fowls. She spent contented hours at her piano and over her home mail, which, until lately, she had rather neglected. And she did not complain of the increasing heat, nor of the compulsory imprisonment indoors during the long days. She had plenty of resources within herself, and her high spirits never flagged. Any idea of going to the hills apparently had not occurred to her, and Coventry, whose theory was that as long as she kept her health a wife's place was with her husband, prudently did not suggest it. Not that he would have actually distrusted her away from him, but his peace of mind must have suffered acutely, knowing that she was making friendships and joining in amusements that he could not supervise; for undoubtedly Trixie would enjoy herself without reflection wherever she might be, and then there was always the fear of people talking, which held a kind of nightmare niche in his imagination.

It was just at this peaceful period that an invitation came for him to join the camp of a well-known sportsman on a tiger-shooting expedition, an opportunity that no man, however uxorious a husband—and especially a man like Coventry, with whom sport had always been a passion—could easily resist without regret. And yet he hesitated. He could not honestly feel that he did not want to go, and yet he could have wished that Markham had not remembered him, had not thought of giving him this tempting chance, or that the letter had miscarried on the way and never reached him.

When he opened the letter he and Trixie were seated at their early breakfast in the veranda, attended by a greedy and devoted gathering of pets. Two well-disciplined fox terriers watched in quivering impatience for scraps of toast, obediently oblivious of a pair of Persian kittens that clawed and mewed and sprang in unmannerly fashion; a noisy green parrot in a dome-shaped cage; a monkey that jumped and jabbered on the back of the memsahib's chair; a tame squirrel that darted to and fro with bead-like eyes and feathery tail, even a greater trial to the dogs than the Persian kittens. Trixie worshipped animals and children; indeed, she had one day scandalised the general's wife by declaring, most immodestly as that lady considered, that she intended to have twenty babies, but, meanwhile, she could content herself with dogs and cats and monkeys.

Coventry threw the letter across the table to his wife; he half hoped she would read it with dismay, and show reluctance that he should accept the invitation. This, he felt, would give him just the excuse he wanted to refuse it, would put a definite obstacle in the way of acceptance instead of his being left at the mercy of conflicting inclinations. He watched her read the letter, but her expression did not cloud; on the contrary, it brightened.

"Oh, George!" she cried, looking up at him with shining eyes, "how lovely for you, and how I wish I could come too! I'd give anything to ride an elephant all day, and see tigers charge, and hear them roar, and then wear a necklace of their claws!"

"Markham won't have women on his shoots. He says it degrades the sport to the level of garden party games!" said Coventry.

"Oh, what a pig he must be!"

"Anyway, it would be far too rough for you, and the heat would be awful in tents. I'm not at all sure that I like the idea of it myself."

"You surely can't mean that you are dreaming of refusing?" cried Trixie, in amazed reproach. "Of course, you must go. He asks you to wire, so you must answer at once. Shall I get a telegraph form?"

"I'm not particularly keen on going," he said, with affected carelessness.

"I don't believe it! I am sure you are aching to wire and say you are coming. If you are pretending that you don't want to go because you think I shall be lonely, you can put that out of your head at once. I shan't miss you a bit."

She in her turn was acting the hypocrite. In reality her heart had sunk a little as she read the letter. She knew she should miss George very much, that she would feel lonely, dull, and rather helpless without him, and she suddenly recognised that she leaned on him mentally a good deal more than she had been aware of hitherto. Also that his interest in and sympathy with all her little schemes and undertakings had meant much to her. Secretly she had been surprised at her own acceptance of the daily monotony and lack of excitements, and wondered vaguely why she was not bored; and now the knowledge came to her with almost startling effect that it was because of George's constant presence. She looked at him with new attention—he was in uniform, for he had just returned from early parade—and a little glow of pride in his appearance kindled in her heart. Certainly she had a very handsome husband, and, moreover, he was kind and good and faithful, even if his ideas of propriety were somewhat tedious and old-maidish, and he was inclined to be jealous and over-particular. After all, he knew the world; his experience had been long and wide, and he had no great reason to trust either men or women. Trixie seldom thought of the first Mrs. Coventry. The old story had not troubled her; hardly had she regarded it as real. The whole of George's past life was more or less unreal to her, for the reason, perhaps, that he had never spoken of more than casual happenings, or small reminiscences connected with his mother, now dead, and his sister, who had taken up missionary work in the slums of London.

In addition, Trixie was a person who contemplated the present and the immediate future to the exclusion of retrospection, partly because she was so young and had all her life before her, and again because it was her nature. She neither looked back nor far forward. Yet now a glimmering of what her husband might have suffered in the past disturbed her self-engrossment, and caused her to feel inadequate and humble, possessed with a helpless regret that drove her to an unselfish desire to conceal her own feelings over this question of his absence. Her apparent anxiety that he should accept Mr. Markham's invitation was construed by Coventry to mean that she was more or less unaffected by the prospect of his absence, and, half hurt and half resentful, he said a little captiously:

"Well, if you want to get rid of me, of course I'll go."

"You know very well you are dying to go," answered Trixie, with good humour; "and it will do you good. All these years at home you've only been able to shoot pheasants and rabbits and little birds; and what are they compared with tigers?"

"It's much more difficult to shoot a snipe than a tiger," argued Coventry perversely.

"All the better. You'll be able to bring me back several dozen skins, and heaps of claws, and plenty of those funny little bones that make into brooches and are supposed to bring such good luck."

"How did you know about the bones?" he asked, rather to delay the making of a decision at the moment than because he wished to hear.

"Mother has one—not that it ever brought her any luck, poor dear, unless it was getting me married; and I suppose Gommie, at any rate, would call that good luck! Guy Greaves told me about the bones, too, and he's going to give me one when he shoots his first tiger. He was to have come back yesterday, wasn't he? Was he on parade this morning?"

"Yes," said Coventry.

The sudden mention at this juncture of young Greaves made Coventry's heart contract with a spasm of jealous apprehension.

"I hope," he said, with injudicious haste, "that, if I do go on this shoot, you won't let that boy hang round the bungalow and follow you about all over the place while I am away."

Trixie flushed. "So that is why you hesitated about going?" she asked him ominously. "Perhaps you would like me to say 'Not at home' to visitors and refuse every invitation while you are not here?"

"Trixie, don't be foolish!" He regretted having voiced his feelings. It had put him in a false position. Now he must either accept the invitation, or refuse it and remain under the suspicion that he would not leave his wife because he feared he could not trust her to behave becomingly. "Of course, I know you would not do anything really wrong, but you are so careless about appearances, and people don't take circumstances into consideration. Why should they? They wouldn't know or remember that you have known Greaves nearly all your life. They would only say that he was in love with you, and that you were encouraging him. You can't be too careful in India, where we all know each other, and live, so to speak, on the house-tops."

"Then you wouldn't mind how much I went about with Guy so long as nobody was any the wiser?"

"Yes, of course I should; but I naturally should not put the same construction on it that people would who did not know you."

"Perhaps you had better not go, then," said Trixie sweetly; and she began to play with the monkey and pet the kittens, and throw scraps to the dogs. Then she rose, flourishing a bunch of keys. "I must go and fight with the cook," she announced. "His bill for charcoal is preposterous. The other women tell me we use four times what we ought—or pay for it, at any rate—and, of course, that won't do, will it, George?"

He ignored the appeal, and with ostentatious indifference she strolled into the house, jingling her keys. The dogs followed her, and Coventry sat in moody perplexity, remorseful, heavy hearted. The kittens began to clamber all over the table, the monkey helped himself from the sugar-basin, and the parrot rent the air with jealous abuse in Hindustani. Oblivious to it all, Coventry lit a cigarette and stared out at the dry compound. He was reflecting that he ought not to have married again at his age and with his temperament—or that at least he should have chosen a sedate and serious spinster, if not some gentle widow, who would have caused him no anxiety, no heart disturbance, as did Trixie—one whom he could have left without a qualm for any call of pleasure or of duty. And Trixie was to be pitied. She might have been far happier with a young husband as gay and heedless, and as irresponsible, as herself. They would have gained their experiences, have "worried through" together, come out none the worse for ups and downs and disagreements, having the same outlook on life, and with youth and tastes in common. He wondered if she repented her marriage, if he bored her, if perchance she really preferred the company, say, of young Greaves, to his own? The thought tortured him. He felt he could not go away and leave her. He would only be miserable, unable to enjoy himself, thinking of her all the time, picturing her riding, driving, laughing with that idiotic boy, while the station smiled and whispered, amused, yet commiserating the absent husband.

Markham's letter had fallen from the table and lay open at his feet. He picked it up and read it through again, and the call of the jungle stirred his blood with unwelcome temptation. It was such years since he had heard the whisper of an Indian forest and the hot, dry crackle of tall grass, since he had swayed on the back of an elephant, alert and ready for the sight of a great striped beast, and known the fierce excitement of "sitting up" over a "kill," waiting breathless, motionless, for the first faint sound of a stealthy tread.

Trixie came back. She slapped the kittens and scolded the monkey, and then looked over George's shoulder.

"Well," she said cheerfully, "have you made up your mind? If you're going, you ought to overhaul your guns and rifles without any delay. You'd have to start in a day or two. You see, he says the 15th at the latest." She pointed with a pink, tapering finger to a paragraph in the letter.

He moved restlessly. "I must think it over," he said, with some irritation.

"All right. But you can't keep Mr. Markham waiting indefinitely for your answer. There are hundreds of men who would give their eyes and ears and noses for the invitation. I only wish I could dress up as a man, and stick on a moustache, and go instead of you."

Anger seized him, engendered by his mingled feelings of reluctance and desire to take advantage of the chance.

"Hang!" he exclaimed, rising to his feet. "I'll go, and take the consequences."

"What consequences?" asked Trixie. "George, you weren't really serious when you talked about Guy Greaves just now? You don't really think you couldn't leave me for a fortnight in case I should get into mischief, and do something that would make you and me seem ridiculous?"

"You don't understand," he argued hotly.

"Then will you explain?"

"I have tried to, but you can't see my point of view. It isn't that I don't trust you, Trixie; I know you don't mean any harm; but if you make yourself conspicuous with other men you can't expect people not to talk and think the worst, and I can't bear that you should be a subject for scandal."

"But why should you imagine I am going to give anybody cause to talk directly your back is turned? I should do nothing while you are away that I wouldn't do while you are here."

"That's just it!" he said, with some excitement. "If you ride and drive all over the place with young Greaves, and let him come and sit here for hours, as you did before he went on leave, there is bound to be gossip."

"But *you* know that there's nothing in it," she argued plaintively. "You have said so. Isn't that enough?"

Then her heart smote her. She knew she was teasing him, making it more difficult for him to go away with a light heart to enjoy the shoot; and while she considered his attitude absurd, she made up her mind she would humour his scruples and sink her own opinion in favour of the circumstances. Poor dear old George! He was such a prude, so dog-in-the-mangerish, so prone to make a silly fuss about nothing. Yet, if it really worried him to think that she and Guy might lead people to imagine they were lovers, she would give in to him and promise anything he liked. She wanted him to have some pleasure; she was conscious that her notions of enjoyment were not his, and she felt it would be more than "beastly"—to use her own term—not to help him now to get off on this tiger shoot with a mind at ease.

She came round the table and perched herself on his knee, winding a soft arm about his neck.

"Will it make you happy, old George, if I promise not to go out with Guy while you are away, and not to let him come here when I am alone?"

He pressed her to him in fond compunction, overwhelmed with tender feeling for her, recognising gladly the generous impulse that had prompted her concession.

"Darling, I don't ask you to promise anything. I only want you to remember that you are a married woman, and to guard your name and reputation as something sacred. You have only to think a little, and not expect other people to be as charitable and unsuspicious of evil as you are yourself."

She kissed him lightly on the forehead. "I will think and remember the whole time," she reassured him. "You needn't feel one bit afraid. I shall have heaps to do without bothering about men. I'm going to hem dozens of dusters, and the Padre's wife has promised to teach me no end of cooking, so I shall keep her to her word. You'll be back before I can turn round."

"How can I leave you?" he said, with passionate reluctance.

She laid on the breakfast-table a piece of paper she had brought from the bungalow.

"Here's a telegraph form," she announced cheerily, "and my fountain-pen. I'm going to write out the wire for you. What shall I say?" She shifted her position and began to trace the words: "'Accept with many thanks starting soon as possible.' How's that?"

"Well," he said grudgingly, "I suppose I'd better go."

"You *are* going," Trixie told him; "and when you are there you will bless your wife for making you go." She referred to Markham's letter and added the address. Then she rose and summoned with a call a lurking orderly, and gave him the form, with some money hitherto secreted in the palm of her hand. "Take that to the post office," she commanded him in halting Hindustani.

In silence they watched the man leave the compound with alert, important progress, and Coventry gave a sigh of resignation.

"You young bully!" he said in mock reproach.

"You old idiot!" she retorted, laughing, and bustled back to grapple with her housekeeping.

Chapter 10

The River

After that there followed a period of unusual activity in the Coventry's bungalow. Guns and rifles were overhauled, ammunition ordered, boxes and cupboards were ransacked for garments suited to the jungle.

Trixie entered keenly into all the preparations. She seldom did anything by halves; and she might almost have been joining in the expedition herself so lively was her interest in every detail. She asked endless questions concerning camps and elephants and tigers, and she listened breathless to all that George could tell her of the fascinations of the jungle. She dragged books on sport from the musty shelves of the club library, and read them with genuine enjoyment during two long, hot afternoons.

Coventry to the last was more or less reluctant to leave her; but she ignored his hesitation, and when the hour of departure came she drove with him gaily to the railway station, and with a cheerful, smiling face saw him off by the night mail.

It was when she returned to the empty bungalow that her spirits sank. The rooms were so silent, save for the tiny trumpeting of mosquitoes in the corners; the atmosphere felt so close, and there was a smell of musk rat that was nauseating. Until dawn brought comparative coolness she lay awake, turning restlessly, hearing the desperate cry of the brain-fever bird, and the monotonous thrumming of a stringed instrument in the servants' quarters at the end of the compound. She wondered if natives ever slept save during the spell of rest they claimed in the middle of the day, when a drowsy peace descended everywhere.

With a sense of dismay that hitherto she had held in check, she contemplated the coming fortnight. How boring it would be to have to "think and remember" the whole time that she must be careful to give no cause for gossip! True, she had her household and her livestock, and her linen and store cupboards to occupy her mornings, and she could read and sleep through the succeeding hot hours; but what of the evenings?

For the first week she got on well enough. She snubbed Guy Greaves and other eager slaves who would willingly have placed their time, their dog-carts, their ponies—everything that they possessed—

at her disposal. She played in "married" sets of tennis, and dined and consorted with the most domesticated couples in the station, so nervous was she of committing any indiscretion. Every day she wrote to George, accounting for her time; this she felt to be a sort of safeguard against the least false step; and so far there had been nothing connected with her doings that she could not chronicle with a perfectly clear conscience.

So the time dragged on until the evening before the day on which George Coventry was expected to come home.

The heat was now terrific; even tennis had become an effort, and Trixie left the bungalow to keep her engagement in the public gardens, feeling listless and oppressed. The hot weather had begun early this year, there had been no cooling storms to give temporary coolness and relief, and on all sides Trixie heard ominous predictions that "the rains" were going to fail. Not that the prospect disturbed her particularly, for as yet she could not realise its gravity. Only those whose lives have been bound up with India can understand the dread of such a visitation, the anxious watching of the sky, the heaviness of heart when meteorological reports look bad. For a failure, or even a weakness, of the monsoon means grim combat with pestilence and famine, and most dire distress, not only at the time, but afterwards, when fever takes its toll from an enfeebled population. It means strain and over-work for the long-suffering official; everywhere misery, death, and desolation.

After a languid game she dawdled late at the club with a group of people who, like herself, felt unwilling to return to stuffy bungalows and food that must inevitably prove untempting. To-night especially she shrank from the prospect of a solitary dinner and the weary after hours, even though supported by the knowledge that it was her last evening alone.

They all sat outside the club-house on a round masonry platform, talking fitfully, fanned by a make-shift punkah slung between two poles. Gradually two or three married couples bestirred themselves and drove away; a few unattached men who had dinner engagements deserted also, and presently Mrs. Coventry and Mrs. Roy were the only ladies left, with a small attendance of young men—Guy Greaves, two other subalterns, and a home-sick youth who had joined the Civil Service only last winter, and still preserved pathetically a Bond Street air.

Mrs. Roy was young and pretty and light-hearted, but not entirely without guile. Captain Roy had gone away that afternoon on duty, and she did not intend to dine alone. She invited the company to join her at dinner.

"There's lots of food, such as it is," she told them, "and even if we can't eat we can drink champagne with plenty of ice in it."

"I'm afraid I can't come," said Trixie ruefully. She knew that George disapproved of Mrs. Roy.

"Why not?" persisted Mrs. Roy. "Who are you dining with—the missionaries?"

They all laughed.

"I'm not dining with anybody," admitted Trixie, obviously weakening. She longed to join the party and have a little "fling," to laugh and talk nonsense and be amused, as an antidote to all her good behaviour. No letter would have to be written to-morrow to George. She could tell him all about the evening, and make him understand that she had meant and done no harm.

"Then why can't you come? Don't be unsociable," argued Mrs. Roy. "To-morrow we may all be dead of heat apoplexy, or cholera, or snake-bite, or something equally common to this delightful country, and then you'd be sorry you hadn't enjoyed yourself while you had the chance."

"Do say 'Yes,' Mrs. Coventry," sang a chorus of male voices. And after a moment's further hesitation Trixie succumbed.

"I must go back and change, then," she said, and rose.

A little later they all met again in Mrs. Roy's pretty bungalow, and despite the heat and the insects, and, according to Mrs. Roy, the uncertainty of existence in India, they were a festive little party. They chaffed and told stories, and drank iced champagne and smoked cigarettes, and Trixie cast from her all thoughts of her husband's displeasure. Until this evening she had conformed to his wishes with the most strict consideration. She felt she deserved this innocent enjoyment, that it would be really unreasonable of George if he grudged it to her.

She had honestly intended to go home soon after dinner was over, but Mrs. Roy refused to "hear of such a thing."

"Behold the moon!" she exclaimed, a good deal later, as they straggled out into the veranda after a short and boisterous game of cards.

And, indeed, the moon was something to behold—huge, orange-coloured, almost terrifying, hanging heavy in the dusty night. Its lurid light filtered through the foliage of the trees and tinged the haze of the atmosphere with an unearthly radiance.

"I ask you, who could go to bed whilst that great lantern blazes in the sky?" cried Mrs. Roy with mock grandiloquence. "Let us all drive down to the river and go for a row. Wouldn't it be simply perfect?"

And, with others, Trixie agreed. What did it matter? Who cared? There was a sensuous influence in the hot, scented air that stilled her scruples, rendered her reckless. For the moment all the careless, irresponsible gaiety of her girlhood had returned.

The young civilian and one of the subalterns took charge of Mrs. Roy, the other three climbed into Guy Greaves's dog-cart, and they all drove hatless, wrapless, along the deserted, dusty road hedged with dry mud-banks that were tipped with prickly pear and cactus, until the ground began to slope, the wheels of the vehicles sank deep into the heavy, sandy soil, and they were at the river's edge.

There was a little delay while two boats were got ready by sleepy boatmen roused from their huts, a good deal of talk and laughter and argument as to how the party should divide and how far they should row. Finally it was agreed that in an hour's time they should land at the grove of trees that sheltered the Mohammedan cemetery, and that the syces with the traps, and a man to take back the boats, should meet them there.

Trixie found herself afloat alone with Guy Greaves. She did not know if this was due to an accident or to Guy's deliberate manoeuvring. She felt as though she were in a dream as she took the rudder-lines. The second boat shot past them, and the occupants called out foolish jokes and gibes, sprinkled them with water, and left them far behind.

They slid slowly, silently, over the smooth bosom of the holy river, that was burnished with the moonlight. From the distance came the sound of native singing, a faint sound that rose and fell on the warm night air, only to be drowned, as though in protest, by the yells of jackals hunting, closely packed, across the plain.

Then all again was quiet, with a vast and dreamy peace that held the man and woman speechless, like a spell, as the boat slipped through the water, on and on.

Suddenly Guy Greaves stopped rowing. He leaned towards his companion, his young face set and hard, his eyes dark in the moonlight; his hands, holding the oars, were strained and trembling.

"Trixie!" he said in hoarse appeal.

His voice roused her. She looked at him, surprised.

"Why have you been so cruel to me lately? What have I done?"

She felt irritated, helpless. "Don't, Guy. Don't be so silly. I don't know what you mean."

"Oh! I know it's no use. But I must say it; I must tell you." He spoke with quick, nervous emotion. "It isn't as if I'd ever done or said anything since you came out here married to deserve the way you've sat on me lately—or if I have, I didn't know it. I thought I'd been so jolly careful! It hasn't been easy—and it's no good pretending now that I don't care for you, or for you to pretend that you don't know it. You knew it when I was at home last year, and we had such ripping times together. If only I'd been able to afford to marry, wouldn't you have taken me—Trixie? Wouldn't you? Instead of marrying a man old enough to be your great-grandfather!"

The boy had lost his head; his words came with passionate bitterness.

"Guy, be quiet!" Trixie broke in, distressed and alarmed. "You must be mad to talk like this."

He paid no heed. "No, I'm not mad—unless, perhaps, with wretchedness. I could stand it all as long as you treated me as a pal, and were kind, and let me do things for you. But you suddenly kicked me off like an old shoe, and, as far as I can see, for no reason whatever. I want to know," he went on doggedly, "what I've done."

"You haven't done anything," she hastened to tell him. "It's all your silly imagination. Do, for goodness' sake, go on rowing; we shall never catch up the others before they land."

He sat motionless, waiting.

"Guy—you *must* row on. I'll tell you nothing while you behave like this. It's beastly of you. Look—we're floating to the other side of the river! Guy, do be sensible!"

That was what she had said to him last year at home, when he had "talked nonsense" at a dance before he had to sail for India. They both remembered it now. In her agitation she clutched at the rudder-lines confusedly, and the boat almost swung round. He steadied it with the oars, but he did not go on rowing.

"Would you have married me if it had been possible?" he persisted, though now more calmly.

There was a long pause. The boat moved sideways, gravitating towards the farther bank, nearing ridges of sand and islets of brushwood and rubbish, mysterious shapes that stuck up sharp and fantastic in the moonlight. Something swished past, rippling the water with swift cleavage—a long, black water-snake hurrying to its refuge. And a mighty splash broke the stillness—a crocodile disturbed from its stupor on a sandbank.

"No," said Trixie in a low, tense voice, "I would not have married you. I think I could never have married anybody but George."

The truth had come to her, here on the river in the moonlight, with sudden and overpowering force. She loved her husband, loved him with all her generous, impulsive heart—and this in spite of his strict views and old-fashioned opinions, his tiresome jealousy, his age! And yet at this very moment she was doing something that, if he could know of it, would hurt and anger him and shake his trust in her, destroy all his pleasure in his holiday, perhaps create a rupture between them that never could be healed! What a fool she had been to dine with Mrs. Roy, to allow herself to be dragged into this idiotic escapade. And here was Guy behaving like a lunatic because she was alone with him on the river in the middle of the night. How could she ever explain it all to George and persuade him to forgive her?

Before her mental vision rose her husband's handsome, careworn face—the keen grey eyes, the dark hair frosted at the temples; and with it came remembrance, realisation of all he must have suffered in the past. How often he had told her that she had restored to him his trust in womanhood, had made him happy when all hope of happiness had seemed denied him.

In a measure she had failed him, too. He would be certain to hear of to-night's folly, even if she told him nothing about it herself. The only thing to do was to get home as quickly as possible.

Guy Greaves sat opposite to her, obdurate, motionless, thinking only of himself and his stupid, boyish adoration, which was nothing compared with the love of a man experienced and tried. She felt she hated Guy, and all the superficial view of life that he represented to her penitent soul.

"Oh, go on—go on!" she cried in frightened desperation. "I must get home. I ought never to have come. I can't bear it. If you don't row, I'll never speak to you again."

He took up the oars with reluctance. She pulled the rudder-lines again, first one, then the other. The boat shot crookedly, with a shivering shock, on to a sandbank, and stuck fast.

Young Greaves said "Damn!" and Trixie screamed. She stood up.

"For God's sake sit down!" implored Guy, in fear that she might spring from the boat, a hideous thought of lurking crocodiles flashing through his mind.

She sank back to her seat, mute, apprehensive, while he tried vainly to refloat the boat.

"Give me an oar. Let me help," she said. He passed it to her. They used all their strength without avail.

"Shout!" she ordered him. "The others may hear you and come back."

He obeyed her, and the sound echoed wide and far across the water. But the only answer was the hooting of an owl in some bushes on the bank, and the scrambling of some startled little creature near them in the sand.

"We shall be here all night!" she cried, despairing.

He did not answer. All his attention was concentrated on his efforts to release the boat.

Actually how long it stuck there neither of them knew. The moon sank lower, glowing, molten; myriads of mosquitoes beat about them, bit their faces, hands, and feet; the river seemed as stagnant as a pool.

Trixie felt paralysed, as in a nightmare. What if they were kept prisoners till the dawn—even longer—even till George should have returned to the bungalow and found her absent?

All at once, with a lurch, the boat shot free, and Trixie burst into tears of relief.

Guy Greaves felt almost hysterical himself. "It's all right now, Trixie. Don't cry." He spoke with cheerful reassurance. "I'll row hard, and we shall catch the others up in no time."

"They must have landed long ago," she quavered. "Can't we go back to the starting-place? It must be nearer."

"But the traps were to meet us at the grove," he reminded her. "We should have to walk all the way home if we went back, and that would take ever so much longer."

"Supposing the others haven't waited," she suggested nervously. "It would be just like them. They can't all get into the same trap, and they'd take yours and leave us to fish for ourselves without caring twopence!" Her agitation rendered her petulant and pessimistic. "You know how thoughtless and inconsiderate Mrs. Roy can be. That is why George can't bear her."

"Oh, nonsense! Mrs. Roy's dog-cart holds four at a pinch, if they let the syce follow. Even if they did take my trap, they'd send it back to meet us. Anyway, don't worry about that till we get there."

He rowed harder than ever, infected in spite of himself by Trixie's forebodings; and he felt hardly surprised to see only the boatman awaiting them on the rough little landing-stage.

"What did I tell you!" said Trixie, a catch of despair in her voice.

"They wouldn't wait down here," he said, as he helped her out of the boat. "Are the sahibs up above in the grove?" he inquired of the man.

The answer was given with drowsy indifference. "I know not. The order was given to wait for this boat, and take it back with the other."

They stumbled on up the slope that was steep and uneven, Trixie clinging to Guy, her breath coming fast and audible. "Do coo-ee," she urged him, "I feel I must know if they're there." He obeyed her. His voice rang clear through the trees and over the river, but echo was all the reply it received.

In disconsolate silence they reached the flat ground at the top of the cliff, and plunged into the mysterious gloom of the grove. A weak little breeze had arisen, wandering through the trees, like a sighing soul that could not escape from the burial place; here and there they could see the dim outlines of tombs, dome-shaped, or flat-topped and square, touched by the light of the moon that filtered down through the foliage.

"They are not here. They have gone," said Trixie hopelessly.

"They are outside, waiting on the road," said Guy Greaves.

But they were not. When the pair emerged from the grove they found the road empty and silent, not a sign of a trap or anything living, except a great owl that swooped over the road and across the unfertile plain beyond with an unearthly hoot, as though mocking their plight.

"Come along," said Trixie firmly, "we must walk. If they do send the trap back to meet us so much the better, but we can't wait here on the chance."

The road was unmetalled and the ruts were deep. Without further parley they started, trudging through the dust, engrossed in their own emotions. The boy felt that by his lack of self-control he had jeopardised all future friendship with his idol, and his young heart was heavy with distress, also with resentment; for it seemed to him that Trixie thought he was to blame for their predicament. Barring that asinine outburst of his, which he deeply regretted, he did not see why she should be so perturbed—not only perturbed, but actually frightened. If anyone should be spiteful enough to gossip, the whole thing could be clearly explained in two minutes. Why, in the old days Trixie would have been the first to enjoy such a harmless adventure. A question crept into his mind and filled him with angry concern: Was she afraid of her husband? He recalled certain tales of his colonel's first marriage, chiefly the one that Coventry's jealous restrictions had goaded his wife into bolting with some other fellow. Aunt Marion Greaves had once hinted as much in his hearing, and others had said the same. He stepped along burning with rage at the notion that Trixie was bullied, devising impossible schemes to shield and defend her from trouble with Coventry over to-night's escapade.

Trixie herself was practically oblivious of his presence. She did not observe that he walked a little ahead, his motive being to make sure that she trod on nothing suggestive of reptiles; once he did notice a thin black line that wriggled from the dust in front and disappeared beneath a cactus clump. Luckily she did not see it; she was absorbed in her desire to find herself safe within her home, torn as she was with repentance for her backsliding, dreading as she did the confession she would have to make to George. Guy startled her presently by an abrupt question:

"Why are you in such a funk?" he asked, as though the words had been jerked from his lips against his will.

"What?" said Trixie, with an effort. "What did you say?" She only knew he had spoken, without catching the words.

"I only said, why are you so awfully worried about—about all this? There can't be any scandal when the whole thing was simply an accident."

"It wasn't an accident my going out with all you silly idiots in the middle of the night!" said Trixie crossly. "And if people do talk and say nasty things about our being left behind it will be my own fault, and I shall deserve it. Anyhow, it has taught me a lesson I shan't forget in a hurry."

"Oh, rot! What can they say? And why should you care. Look here, Trixie," he burst out with imprudent impetuosity, "is it that you're in a funk of what *the colonel* will say or do? For God's sake, tell me if he bullies you. We all know what happened about his first wife."

There was an ominous pause. His pulses beat quickly, the noise of their footsteps crunching the dust sounded loud in his ears. He wished he had let the subject alone.

Then he heard Trixie say in a cold, contemptuous voice: "Perhaps you will tell me what you all know?"

In nervous excitement he stammered his answer. "Why, that he drove her into—into leaving him. Never gave her a chance, wouldn't listen."

And in spite of the anger she felt towards Guy for his outrageous presumption, Trixie's heart sank lower than ever. She knew so little of the history of George's first marriage—had refused to hear when her mother and "Gommie" had wanted to tell her. Never once had she questioned her husband about the divorce, and naturally no one had mentioned it to her in India, until now this blundering boy had raked up the talk he had heard. A horrible doubt assailed her. Could it be true that George had behaved without mercy, had not been entirely blameless as she had always believed? If so, what might she expect herself when he knew she had not only flown in the face of his wishes, but had been absent nearly all night with Guy Greaves, the one individual, harmless youth though he was, with whom he had begged her not to make herself conspicuous during their separation—Guy, over whom they had almost quarrelled! Hurt and annoyed she was sure her husband would be, but what if, as well, he "would not listen, would not give her a chance?"

Her vexation of mind, her disturbance of conscience, the annoying delay, the scene with Guy on the river, had all combined to harass her nerves and distort her perceptions; and now her companion's perturbing suggestion filled her with dread. Nevertheless her spirit rose up in defence of her husband.

"You know nothing about it," she told Guy severely. "How dare you quote gossip to me! And as to your insinuation about George's behaviour towards me, it only just proves how little you know him."

"They why make such a fuss?" he argued morosely. He did not believe that Trixie was telling the truth.

"Look here, Guy!" She stopped in the middle of the road, and compelled him to turn and face her. "If you weren't such an old friend, and if I didn't know you were a good sort, I should never speak to you again. As it is, you must know we can't be on quite the same terms any more. But I should like you to understand, once and for all, that I love my husband, and because I love him it makes me wretched to think that I should have done anything to vex him. I have broken a promise and behaved like a senseless fool. Of course I shall tell him the whole thing, and I am not in the least afraid that he won't forgive me. But that doesn't make me feel any the less ashamed of myself."

All the same, despite her brave words, Trixie was frightened as well as ashamed, and in her heart she knew that Guy had not only divined her fear, but that he shared it himself acutely.

It was a blessed relief to them both to catch sight at this moment of a dark object moving slowly towards them along the road—Guy Greaves's trap, sent back by the rest of the party to meet them. In silence they got into the trap and jolted along the uneven road till they reached the metalled highway; then they spun swiftly, unhindered, towards the station.

Chapter 11

The Jungle

The sun beat fiercely down on the bed of the river, now dry save for streamlets meandering among the boulders, and encircling patches of sand that were dotted with birds of the long-shanked, long-billed brotherhood. It seemed hard to believe that a few weeks hence this arid, stone-strewn area would be swept by a mighty, tempestuous flood, rushing down from the hills in a volume so vast that nothing could stem its advance. Now the boulders shone round and smooth, and blinding white in the midday heat. They might have been cannon balls hurled by some Titan race in the ages past from the amphitheatre of hills at some foe in the valley beneath. The islets of sand sparkled like gold; indeed, gold dust was known to be mixed with their grains, though as yet whence it came was a secret no man had discovered; at least, if he had, the secret was kept by enchantment. There were stories of venturesome pilgrims, returning from far-away shrines in the mountains, found dead by the road that led back to the world, with nuggets of gold on their persons; no one had lived to return to the spot where he found them.

The straggling line of elephants, lurching in leisurely progress across the bed of the river, showed like black blots among the boulders. The animals felt their footing with careful precision, splashing through narrow streams, avoiding the stretches of sand that might prove to be death-traps for ponderous beasts, tearing up wisps of scrub with their trunks and beating them free of dust before putting them into their mouths, or flinging them far in disdain.

Captain Coventry's elephant brought up the rear of the little procession. He sat idly back in his howdah, his guns and his rifles stacked before him. His thoughts had wandered from river-beds, elephants, "kills," and tigers; for the tents of the camp, gleaming white in a grove of trees on the opposite bank, had attracted his eye, and he was hoping to find a letter from Trixie awaiting him there. His face was burnt by the sun to the hue of a brick, he looked lean and hard and in fine condition. The fortnight in camp had been all to his taste—congenial companions, capital sport, the arrangements as perfect as only a hunter such as his host could have made them.

This morning the camp had moved, therefore sport on the march had been varied. Two pad elephants carried the game—spotted deer, jungle fowl, partridge, a wild boar with tushes like ivory sickles, and, chief of all, a magnificent panther, shot by Coventry as it lay stretched along the branch of a tree, watching with wicked green eyes the party of sportsmen filing beneath.

Coventry's leave was nearing its close. In a couple of days he was due to return to the station, and he sometimes surprised himself counting the hours. But he did not intend to desert "the shoot" before the appointed time, especially since the object in moving the camp to-day was to get within reach of a man-eating tiger whose terrible doings had scared all the people for miles around. The inhabitants of the little jungle villages were almost paralysed with fear, their crops were neglected, they dared not take out their cattle to graze; the brute was as active by day as by night, and had even been known to come into a hut and drag out his victim. From all accounts he was not of the usual mangy type that, enfeebled by age, finds man a much easier prey than the deer or the buffalo; he was described by the people as a creature of monstrous proportions, in the prime of life, and possessed with a spirit that was without doubt of the devil, since he slew beasts for caprice or amusement, and human beings for food. Many were "the sahibs" who had sought to destroy him, on foot, from howdahs, from seats in the trees; in vain had bullocks and goats and buffalo calves been tied up as bait; even the ghastly remains of his meals had been watched. Yet still he went free, the "slayer," the "striped one," the "lord of the jungle." (No villager mentions the tiger by name, for fear of ill-luck.)

As the sportsmen arrived in their camp they were met by a terrified group, a deputation of wretched, half-naked people who had come from a hamlet near by to report yet another disaster. They waited while the sahibs got down from the elephants and stretched their cramped limbs, and then they approached with humble yet eager appeal.

"Highness, protector of the poor, father and mother, we are humble folk," wailed the spokesman, prostrating himself at their feet, a mummified object with rags round his head and his loins. "Thy slaves do entreat thee to slay the 'shaitan' that stalketh by day and by night. No one is safe. Only last night did the evil one fall on the wife of my nephew as she went forth to draw water from the well. In front of our eyes did he spring out and seize her and carry her off in his jaws; and when her husband ran in pursuit, like a fool, with curses and cries, did

ALICE PERRIN

the evil one pause and look back. And he threw down the woman and smote the man also, then bore the woman away to the jungle. If it should be the sahibs' pleasure to know that this dust speaks but truth, will we guide the huzoors to the spot where my nephew lies hurt unto death in the village. Maybe he is dead by now."

Again the deputation salaamed, as one man, to the ground, then stood gazing at the sahibs in hopeful anticipation.

"We'd better go and see if there's anything to be done for the wretched beggar," suggested Markham; "and if the tiger should be about and come for us, so much the better; we'll polish him off."

All four "sahibs" were hot and hungry and thirsty. Coventry was hungry for his letters, as well as for his breakfast. But without further delay they followed the squalid, excited little band in single file along a jungle track, their rifles under their arms. They passed through a sea of feathery grass that grew high above their heads, and on among dense bamboo thickets and tangled scrub. They were close to the edge of the forest, and the rustle of the tree-tops in the fierce west wind was unceasing. Their boots sank deep into hot, dry dust; sometimes startled animals darted across the track almost between their feet—little hog deer, squirrels, hares, jackals that slunk noiselessly into the grass. The harsh calling of pea-fowl, the chatter of monkeys, the screams of green parrots resounded above them. The heat was like that of a furnace; it was a blessed relief to emerge from the close-bound path on to a clearing in front of the village. It was a pathetic little patch of habitation, the people members of a jungle tribe not far removed from aborigines; just a cluster of mud-built dwellings thatched with grass, a shallow tank covered with green slime, in which pigs and buffaloes wallowed; refuse was scattered about, and on a rudely constructed platform under the usual peepal tree a few aged human beings, wasted with fever and poverty, sat huddled together; naked children with swollen stomachs played at their feet, and mangy pariah dogs met the arrivals with furious barking. It was just such a place as a man-eating tiger could persecute at his pleasure.

Coventry never forgot the sickening scene that followed. He and his friends were conducted with noisy ceremony into a hut that already seemed crowded with people; women were wailing, the smell and the heat and the dimness of the interior were stifling in their effect, and on a low string bedstead lay a twisted form partially covered with rags.

The patriarch who had led the deputation to the camp stepped forward full of importance.

"Behold, sahibs, this is the doing of the destroyer!"

To the horror of the Englishmen, before they could check him, he lifted the mask of the unfortunate victim by the nose, and held it poised in the air for a moment before he replaced it. Mercifully the man was dead, only just dead, however; he had lived through the night and into the day with the whole of his face, from the scalp to the chin, torn away by the tiger.

"WHAT EXTRAORDINARY BEGGARS THESE JUNGLE people seem to be! I believe that old brute this morning would have lifted off that poor devil's face just the same if we'd got there while he was alive; in fact, I don't think he knew he was dead." The speaker, one of the shooting party, was a young man fresh to India, and this his first experience of the jungle had been full, for him, of excitement and wonder.

"Probably not," said Markham; "the callousness of the Oriental does strike one as pretty brutal sometimes, but it's just an acceptance of misfortune ingrained in them by their religion. In their own way they are charitable and kind-hearted, and they are often brave to rashness. When you come to think what that village has endured, you'd imagine there'd be hardly a sane inhabitant left."

The murmur of voices reached Coventry's brain as from a distance, though the two who were talking were only a few paces from him. He lay half asleep on a long camp chair in the shade, Trixie's letters clasped in his hand—a three days' budget brought out by runners from the nearest point of postal communication. Trixie was well, she had written, but she missed him, the time had seemed long, she was glad it was nearly over. Holding her letters he dreamed, as he dozed, of their meeting, while the murmur of voices went on. . . Then as he stirred he caught snatches of talk through his dreams, now distinct, now connected, as drowsiness lifted.

The boy was saying: "You must have seen some curious things in your time, I suppose, sir?" He spoke with the awe and respect of youth for age and experience, as though Markham might be a hundred years old at the least.

Coventry listened, amused, and kept his eyes closed. He knew that if Markham chose, he could tell some odd stories. He lay quiet and listened.

"Well, yes, I suppose I have," Markham said musingly; and Coventry heard him knocking his pipe on his chair before he refilled it. The words and the sound were hopeful. Coventry lay quiet and listened.

ALICE PERRIN

"Is there any truth in the tales about children being carried away, and brought up by wolves in the jungle?"

"Undoubtedly. I once saw one myself; in fact, I'm sorry to say I shot the poor creature."

The boy gasped. Markham went on:

"We were out at the foot of the hills after bear, and coming back to camp one evening something jumped out of the long grass and I fired. You see, I don't often miss, and the thing was dead when we picked it up. It wasn't a monkey, as we thought at first; it was a wild man, covered with hair, and evidently it had always gone on its hands and knees."

"And what did you do?" came the breathless question.

"Buried it," said Markham briefly, "and said nothing about it."

"Oh, do go on!" urged the boy, enthralled.

Markham laughed. "Let me think," he said indulgently. "Well, last year I went up towards the head of the Ganges to shoot crocodile with a fellow who thought he was going to make money over the skins—selling them for bags and cases, and so on—and one morning a villager came to the camp and asked us to shoot the 'mugger' that had swallowed his wife the day before. He was a washerman, and he said he and the woman had just taken the clothes down to the edge of the river, and had begun to wash them, when a crocodile the size of a boat, as he described it, suddenly rose from the water and dragged his wife under. He declared the beast swallowed her whole then and there, and he seemed awfully put out because she was wearing the whole of her jewellery into which they had put all their savings—as the peasant people are in the habit of doing out here. He added that we should know her by that, and by her long hair. She had the longest hair, he informed us with pride, of any woman in the village. He didn't seem to understand that we might shoot dozens of crocodiles and never come across the one that had swallowed his wife; he kept saying we couldn't mistake it because it was the biggest crocodile that had ever been seen or heard of, and he went away perfectly confident that he would get the jewellery back. Oddly enough next day we did see a monster, and managed to bag him, and when we cut him open there was the wretched woman in his inside—jewellery, and long hair, and all! The whole village turned out and salaamed to us as if we had been gods, and they became such a nuisance we had to move on."

"Hullo, Markham! Yarning?" Another member of the shoot came out of his tent fresh from a snooze, and flung himself into an empty chair. "What is it? Ghosts, or tigers, or murders, or witchcraft?"

"It's your turn now," said Markham good-temperedly; "tell him the most hair-raising tale you can think of, and give me a rest. As a policeman you ought to know plenty."

"Plenty," replied the policeman, and yawned. "But I can't remember any just now. It's too hot, and I'm too sleepy."

"But you must come across such *interesting* things in the bazaars!" said the boy, in a pleading voice. His ambition had been to write, to become an author, to follow in the footsteps of Stevenson, Kipling, and other great masters of romance; but his people, being practical, had scolded and pushed him into the Indian Public Works, and he had no time to use his pen for anything but estimates, reports, and office work, which bored his imaginative soul.

"I did come across an odd little echo of the past only the other day," the policeman admitted with an effort. "I had breakfast one morning with some missionaries in an out-of-the-way corner of my district, and I noticed an old Englishwoman wandering about the compound with an ayah in attendance. She was dressed in grey, with a poke bonnet and full skirts, like the pictures in old *Punches*. They told me she had been found at the time of the Mutiny as a young girl of about fifteen hiding in the jungle wearing native clothes. Nobody knew who she was, and the poor thing couldn't tell them because she was out of her mind, and she had never recovered her reason. She had been handed on to these people by the missionaries they succeeded, and by others before them—and there she had been living for over fifty years, perfectly harmless, costing very little, and only insisting on being dressed in grey and in the fashion of the Mutiny time. If they tried to put her into anything else she only cried and protested pitifully, so they just went on copying the garments, and called her 'Miss Grey.' They can only suppose that her people were killed in the outbreak, and that some faithful servant disguised her and hid her in the jungle, and that then she got lost and went out of her mind with terror."

"And no one will ever know who she was, or what really happened," said the boy, drawing a long breath. "Unless, perhaps, when she is dying it may all come back to her?"

"It's to be hoped it won't," said the policeman, who was not a romanticist.

"It was lucky for 'Miss Grey' that she was found by friends," put in Markham. "By the way, do you remember that case a few years ago——"

Somnolence stole over Coventry's brain once more; the voices droned on and grew fainter, floating away into space; his head drooped again,

ALICE PERRIN

and he found himself back in the station, not at all disconcerted because, with the curious inconsequence of dreams, his bungalow and the racquet court had in some marvellous manner been merged into one. He was playing an excellent game, though the furniture got in the way and Trixie kept trying to stop him. She was saying: "George, do come away—think of the woman in the bazaar"; and a crowd of men standing by shouted in chorus: "Yes, remember, old chap, the woman in the bazaar." Then he fell over a chair in the act of making a wonderful stroke, and as, with a jerk, he awoke, he heard Markham repeating—"woman in the bazaar."

"What on earth are you gassing about?" he said crossly. His head ached, and he felt hot and sticky, in spite of his recent tub.

"The case of that woman whose husband did something he shouldn't connected with money, and got put into prison, and she drifted into one of the big bazaars——"

"What, an Englishwoman?"

"Yes, worse luck. It was some years ago—while you were at home, I suppose; but there was a tremendous fuss made about it at the time, and I believe the Government tried to interfere and to pay her way home, but didn't succeed——"

"That sort of thing isn't so uncommon as you'd think," observed the policeman significantly. "Our service comes up against queer things in that direction."

"Oh, do for Heaven's sake shut up!" exclaimed Coventry, with the captiousness of the newly awakened. "We've had quite enough horrors to last us for one day, at least, what with that business in the village this morning, and now all your infernal reminiscences."

The cause of his dream became clear to him now. While he dozed the conversation around him had recalled to his subconscious mind the unsavoury rumour he had heard in the racquet court one evening—the evening on which, subsequently, he had felt so annoyed with his wife and with young Greaves for staying out late.

"We thought you were asleep," said Markham in a tone of provoking apology.

"So I was, and you woke me up with your jabber."

"It's time you were awake," Markham said, rising. "We ought to be off pretty soon to the machans."

With the courage and skill of his tribe, the shikari had tracked the tiger, and discovered the spot where the mangled remains of the woman lay hidden beneath the bush. This was not far from the village, and during the day the tracker had fashioned *machans*, or rough seats, in the trees for the sahibs, and had tied up a buffalo calf near by as additional bait. In an hour or two the tiger might be on the prowl and return to his hideous meal, though a man-eater's movements are always uncertain—one day, or one night, he may pounce on his prey, and be heard of again next morning five or six miles away; unlike his kindred of more conventional habits, who will kill about every three days, and return as a rule to the carcase two or three times.

It was a long and wearisome wait, sitting cramped and motionless in the trees. Tigers will seldom look up, but the very least noise—a whisper, a movement, a creak of a seat, or the crack of a twig—is sufficient to warn them, and, once suspicious, nothing will tempt them to come within range; they will slink off in silence and slay elsewhere. Coventry and the boy were perched on one platform, their backs against the trunk; lots had been drawn for the seats, and they had been lucky. Their place was just over the bait that was living, and they could see a twisted brown object protruding from under the bush where the tiger had hidden his victim—an arm of the corpse, as the blue glass bangles that still encircled the poor little wrist betokened.

The sun began to go down, flooding the scene with a rose-coloured radiance, and the moon was not due to rise until late. The air was close and the jungle intensely still, save for the humming of countless insects, and sometimes the cry of a peacock, piercing and harsh, in the distance. As the light softened and faded a rustling in the grass told of porcupines that had come out to feed; they seemed, as the boy said afterwards, to be running about like rabbits. Suddenly a shabby little jackal emerged from the undergrowth, noiselessly, with caution; for a moment he stood still and snuffed the air, then he whisked his brush and gave a wild, unearthly yell, repeating it at intervals, and danced and capered in such fantastic fashion that the boy shook with suppressed amusement.

But Coventry stiffened his muscles. He remembered the native belief that some jackals are "pheaows," or providers, by trade, and are supposed to precede the tiger and utter weird cries either to warn him of danger or to announce some find of food. Whether such a belief was based on truth, or whether such conduct was merely the outcome of fear, he knew that the "pheaow's" arrival, with yells and with antics, usually proclaimed the approach of a tiger, and that in all probability it did so now. With a final contortion and a last demoniacal cry the creature fled into covert, and silence again descended, broken only by

ALICE PERRIN

queer little scuffling noises below and the twittering of owls in the trees. Then a troop of brown monkeys came crashing and chattering through the trees, throwing themselves from branch to branch in a state of the wildest excitement; and the buffalo calf, that had so far lain content on the ground, got up and showed symptoms of fear.

Coventry felt certain that the tiger was about, but except for the angry scoldings of the monkeys, and the nervous lowing of the calf, there was nothing to denote the close vicinity of any beast of prey. Time stole on and darkness fell. If the tiger chose to come between the setting of the sun and the rising of the moon there would be little hope of bagging him. The sportsmen had agreed that if he should delay they would wait until the moonlight gave a better chance, or even till the dawn.

Nothing happened, though an intangible vibration in the air kept the human senses tightly strung through the interval of darkness that ensued. Now and then points of light moved over the ground like glow-worms—the eyes of small animals seeking their food.

Then the moon came up, full and serene, the colour of a ripe blood-orange, and threw her molten light upon the scene, till every blade and stick and leaf stood out, sharp and clear, against their own black shadows. The moments seemed interminable, every sound was magnified a hundredfold by the mysterious quiet—the soft fluttering of bats, the breathing of the buffalo calf, the furtive rustles in the grass. Coventry was stiff and tired, he felt half hypnotised; the light was so unnatural, a sort of weird enchantment held the jungle; if a band of sprites and goblins had appeared and danced wildly in a circle he would not have been surprised. He was near the borderland of dreams, and he tried to keep himself awake by thinking of the tiger, of Trixie, of his journey back to the station; but to his annoyance one sentence swung backwards and forwards, like a pendulum, through his brain to the exclusion of everything else: "The woman in the bazaar. The woman in the bazaar." He longed at last to cry it aloud, that he might free his mind from its spell. Why should these words have laid hold of his mind with such provoking persistence? He began to wonder if he had fever, if he had been "touched up" by the sun this morning; certainly his bones were aching and his head felt queer, but that might be due to the wearisome wait and the cramped position. He attempted to find his pulse, but he could not determine whether the beats were too fast, or too slow, or only just normal; and still the sentence clanged to and fro in his brain, "The woman in the bazaar. The woman in the bazaar."

Then above it his ears caught a tangible sound, though at first so stealthy, so faint, as to be almost inaudible. Again it came, this time a little more certain, a careful stir in the grass, a movement so soft and so wary, so light, that it might have been made by a snake. Afterwards silence, a silence charged with supreme suspense and excitement for the watchers alert in the trees; they hardly dared breathe. The buffalo calf strained at its tether, but uttered no sound, the poor little creature was dumb with fear.

Five minutes later something came out of the grass—a long, lithe form that looked grey in the moonlight, that wriggled along the ground with head held low and shoulders humped high; truly a very big tiger, though doubtless the rays of the moon enlarged its appearance unduly. Coventry was reminded of a cat stalking a bird as the beast made a noiseless run towards the buffalo calf and then paused, the muscles rippling under the skin from the large flat head, with ears laid back, to the tip of the tail, that quivered and jerked.

By the laws of sport it was Coventry's shot, for the tiger was nearest to his machan. He caught an agonised whisper of "Shoot, for God's sake!" from the boy, and he raised his rifle.

The weapon felt strangely top-heavy, it swayed in his hands, a mist seemed to rise between him and the sight, and as the report rang out he knew he had missed—missed badly. Almost at once there came other reports from the trees in sharp succession, and a roar of such fury and pain as shook the air, echoing far and near through the forest.

The man-eater's death was terrific. Over and over he rolled, gasping, roaring, biting the earth in his struggles, till with a hoarse, gurgling sigh he lay still, and his crimes were ended.

Chapter 12

In the Bazaar

As was to be expected the camp took a rest next morning. When Coventry left his tent the hot wind had lulled, and the shadows of the trees had stretched half-way across the tract of bare ground that led to the edge of the jungle. He looked a wreck, for the touch of malaria that had ruffled his temper the previous evening, and ruined his chance of killing the tiger, had since developed into a sharp though short attack with the usual ague, and a temperature that would terrify those unacquainted with the common complaint of the country. It is surprising how quickly malarial fever in India can lay a man low, and yet leave him strength sufficient to rise, once it is over, and pursue his general doings as though nothing unusual had happened. Many even continue to work with fever actually on them.

All the way home from the forest Coventry had shivered and grumbled and scolded the rest of the party because he had missed the tiger, and now, though the fever had left him, he felt languid and limp, and peevish, and was hardly the best of companions. On the outskirts of the camp the man-eater's skin was being pegged out to dry surrounded by a chattering concourse. Half the village had been in the camp since daybreak, squatting around the carcase, helping to rub the raw skin with ashes, lauding the sahibs who had slain the destroyer, rejoicing over the death of the enemy. Now they could travel in safety, at least for the present, could tend their crops, and take out their cattle to graze. Their gratitude did not deter them, however, from furtive attempts to annex the whiskers and claws, and lumps of the fat said to be a miraculous cure for rheumatism. There was to be a "tomasha" to-night in the village to celebrate the event, with music and feasting and fireworks, for which, with the usual fate of the benefactor, the sahibs were expected to pay.

Coventry sat dreamily watching the group. The shikari was directing his assistants, abusing them in the loud arbitrary voice that the native so often assumes towards those whom he considers to be his inferiors, holding forth at the same time on the subject of tigers in general. Most of the servants were idling round, joining in the jokes and altercations; and big, blue-black crows skipped boldly into the midst of the gathering, snatching at morsels of flesh and cawing in hoarse excitement. Near at hand some vultures, bald and repulsive, had collected, gloating in expectation of a feast; overhead, in the hard blue sky, kites were soaring, and diving and screaming. In the background the elephants, chained to their posts, showed massive and dark, swinging their heads, beating off the flies with branches of trees or wisps of their fodder held in their trunks.

It was a picturesque scene alluring to a sportsman, yet Coventry was conscious of a sudden satiety of sport and all its appurtenances. He had enjoyed the shoot, had been thoroughly keen throughout, but whether the fever was to blame, or his annoyance at missing the tiger, or the nostalgia for wife and home that had been on the increase the last few days, he now felt he wished never to hear of a tiger or find himself in a machan or a howdah again. He looked at his watch—it had struck him that if he could start to-night he might catch the mail train before the one by which he had meant to travel. Trixie would be so surprised and delighted to see him arrive before he was due; she must have had a dull, empty time, poor child, during his absence. He inferred as much from her letters, though she never complained; Trixie was not one to grumble or whine. He reproached himself for having left her alone, and determined to try and make up to her for his selfishness; should he buy her some nice piece of jewellery when he got back? A new ring. Trixie liked rings, and they looked so well on her pretty pink fingers. Later on he would take her away to the hills and let her enjoy herself just as she liked. Then jealousy stirred in his heart, and whispered: "Of course, within reason." He tried to stifle the whisper, but could not succeed; after all, if Trixie kept well she ought to be happy enough in the plains with him, and her pets, and the riding and tennis.

Markham came out of his tent. "Better, old chap?"

"Yes, better, fairly all right again, thanks. I think I'll go off, though, to-night, all the same. I don't feel quite up to another day's beat with a journey to follow. If I hurry a bit I could catch the mail in the morning."

"You might, but it'll be rather a rush, and you'll get no sleep."

"I can sleep in the train to-morrow."

The desire to start had now become almost an obsession, and he held out obstinately against Markham's well-meant persuasions that he should wait, as previously planned, to benefit by the arrangements already concluded for the convenient return of the party to the nearest junction on the railway. Finally it was settled that he should journey on one of the elephants to a point of habitation where some sort of vehicle could be procured to take him to meet the earlier mail.

Therefore it came about that George Coventry, with his bearer and his baggage, rattled up to his bungalow in a dilapidated "ticca-gharry," hired at the railway station, twelve hours sooner than he was expected. From the moment of his catching, as by a miracle, the earlier mail train, he had been thrilled with sweet impatience, anticipating Trixie's welcome, all her glad surprise, their interchange of little news, the pleasant disturbance of his premature home-coming. Her last letter, which was safe in his breast pocket, together with all the others she had written to him during his absence, had told him how she longed for his return, had declared that the final twenty-four hours would seem longer, more tedious than all the rest. To shorten the time of separation he had jolted and bumped over miles of rough country, enduring horrible discomfort, that he might arrive to-night instead of to-morrow, even if he roused her and the establishment at an inconvenient hour.

Needless to say, his much-needed sleep in the train had been broken and restless. Fever still lurked in his system, and whenever he dozed the beat of the wheels had formed itself into a clockwork song with relentless persistence: "The woman in the bazaar. The woman in the bazaar." He could not get rid of it, could not divert its maddening rhythm. Even now as he got out of the gharry it followed him up the steps and clamoured inside his brain.

The bungalow was silent, dimly lit. A servant lay rolled up in a cotton sheet, like a corpse, across the threshold of the drawing-room door, which was open. Why was the door open? Why were the venetian outer doors not closed and bolted?

The gharry, with his baggage on the roof, the sleepy driver and the miserable ponies, waited at the foot of the veranda steps while the sahib awoke the slumbering servant both with voice and foot.

The man sprang up with the terrified bewilderment of the suddenly awakened native. "Thieves! Murder! Thieves!" he yelled, until he recognised his master, when he bound his turban hastily about his dishevelled head and salaamed in respectful apology. The gharry man was paid, the luggage was deposited in the veranda, and the ramshackle conveyance rattled out of the compound. It all caused a noisy disturbance, and yet Trixie had not been aroused. No questioning call came from her bedroom to know what it all meant. In puzzled apprehension Coventry passed through the drawing-room, where a couple of wall lamps still burned low. Also the light in her bedroom had not been put out. He pushed aside the short curtain and looked into the room. She was not there. The bed was empty, undisturbed.

He returned to the drawing-room and called the bearer. "Where has the memsahib gone to dine?" he asked, realising at the same moment that it was long past the hour for dinner parties to break up.

The man told him blandly that he "believed the memsahib had gone to dine with Captain Roy-memsahib," then added, standing on one foot and rubbing a great toe against the other ankle, that he thought the syce had brought the "tum-tum" back some time ago.

"Call the syce!" said Coventry shortly; and the bearer obeyed, obviously relieved that he was to be questioned no further, since the sahib seemed annoyed.

The syce, a dull but well-intentioned person, could only say that the memsahib had told him to take the cart and the pony home from Roy-mem's bungalow. He did not know why. He also stood on one foot, vaguely apprehensive of the Colonel-sahib's displeasure.

"It was the memsahib's order," he added in hopeful self-exoneration.

"Very well," said Coventry; "go and get the tum-tum ready."

He stood and smoked in the veranda until the trap came round. His mind was in chaos; he could not think connectedly. What was Trixie doing? Had she been taken ill at Mrs. Roy's bungalow? Or had Mrs. Roy been taken ill, and was Trixie staying with her for the night? Either reason, lots of reasons, would explain her absence. Yet beneath the plausible explaining there lurked a dreadful doubt that clutched malevolently at his heart.

He got into his trap and swung rapidly out of the compound. In the light of the moon the dust-white road had a luminous appearance. Coventry remembered that the shortest route to the Roys' bungalow was by the bazaar; he judged that at this time of the night the streets would be clear. He would save a mile at least if he drove through the city.

He came to the outskirts of the great northern native town, a huddle of thatched huts, their thresholds blocked with sleeping forms. Pariah dogs fought and foraged among the rubbish festering in the gutters; their snarls mingled with raucous native coughing, the wail of fretful infants, long echoing yawns.

Then brick walls rose up, dark and irregular, topped with flat roofs, whence rose faint sounds of music and the murmur of voices. Now he had entered one of the main streets of the city that yet was hardly wider than a lane; here and there the road space was rendered still narrower by rough string bedsteads set outside the shops and dwellings, figures, scantily clothed, sprawling upon them. Bats flickered from the roofs across the strip of moonlit sky that was like a lid to the street. The air was stifling; indescribable exhalations, odours of kerosene oil, rancid butter, garlic, sandal-wood, spices, sweating Eastern humanity, thickened and soured the atmosphere, nauseating the white man who drove steadily on through the densely packed clusters of buildings. His head ached, his veins felt as though they must burst in his temples; it seemed to him that he had been driving for hours through this fetid wilderness of bricks, as if he should never emerge into air that was pure and untainted.

The beat of his pony's hoofs echoed loud and regular from wall to wall; otherwise there was a heavy silence as he drove through the silversmiths' quarter, and went past the side street where shoes and sandals were made and sold, a fact proclaimed by a horrible stench of badly cured hide. Suddenly he came upon a patch of light and noise. Some important domestic event was in course of celebration, perhaps a wedding, or the birth of a much-desired son. Rows of little lamps illumined one of the houses, just wicks alight floating in pans of coconut oil, diffusing smoke and smell; a gaudy group of nautch girls singing, twirling, blocked the doorway, and a crowd of musicians and guests and sightseers pushed and jostled each other for some distance down the street. Somehow he got through the flare, and confusion, and clamour, into the dimness beyond, only to find his way barred by a procession of camels padding towards him in shadowy, leisurely progress, groaning and grumbling, escorted by tall men clad in flowing garments and loose turbans, men with snaky black locks, hooked noses and fierce eyes; a camel caravan arriving from the north, laden with merchandise, weary and dusty with arduous travel.

Coventry was forced to halt. It would be impossible in this narrow thoroughfare to get past the long line of beasts burdened with huge bales that swung broadside from their backs. The syce stood up behind him to proffer advice.

That street, he said—the one to the left—would take them into another main road and thence out of the city just as quickly as if they waited for the camel folk to pass.

"It is the street," added the syce casually, "of the dancing women and such-like."

The leading camel, a towering, loose-lipped shape, lurched and lumbered almost on to the trap. Coventry, to avoid the bubbling beast, turned his pony's head, and next moment he was driving down the side street, down "the street of the dancing women and such-like."

Some of the balconies were silent and deserted, others held shadowy shapes; one or two interiors were ablaze with light, and the sound of tinkling music floated from them. There came to his mind the recollection of the hideous story he had heard on the racquet court, now some weeks ago, and he glanced about him with aversion.

The road was rough, scored with ruts and little hollows. Presently the pony stumbled badly, made a desperate struggle to regain his balance, and came down. By an acrobatic leap Coventry avoided being pitched into the road, the syce was shot beneath the seat of the trap, and the pony lay motionless, inert, in helpless submission to fate.

Coventry stood for a moment to steady his senses. The syce crawled from the trap, rubbing his leg, calling encouragement to the prostrate pony, blaming some omen of evil he had observed in the stables only that morning. It was evident, even in the uncertain light, that the trap was badly damaged; both shafts were broken, and Coventry realised that he would drive no farther that night.

By now a small crowd had collected, men and youths chiefly of the Babu persuasion, wearing muslin shawls and embroidered pork-pie caps. They gazed with relish at the spectacle of a white man in a rather undignified quandary, and none of them offered to help while sahib and syce busied themselves with the pony.

Attracted by the little commotion, a woman emerged on to a balcony above, and stood looking down on the group. From the room behind her someone brought out a lamp and held it aloft, so that the woman's face became suddenly visible to those in the street below.

Coventry looked up involuntarily, and his attention was held, riveted, for, though not young, the woman was fair, most strangely fair, in her native dress and tinselled veil; and even the paint that was thick on her eyes and cheeks could not conceal her unusual beauty. Coventry guessed, with a sick conviction, that this was "the woman in the bazaar," the woman of whom he had heard.

Appalled by the certainty, he still peered upward, fascinated yet repelled; and softly the woman laughed—not only laughed, but threw something down that landed, lightly, at his feet. A hoarse murmur of comment went up from the onlookers; one of them, a weedy youth, picked the object up and tendered it to the sahib, exclaiming with insolent politeness: "Thou art favoured, heaven-born."

It was a bunch of crudely artificial violets, drenched with heavy scent that mingled with other odours of the suffocating night. Coventry recoiled as though the sham flowers, with their sickly perfume, had been a deadly reptile. Then he stepped forward, menace in his bearing, and the officious youth, with his companions, shrank, close-packed, from the wrath of the Englishman; only to be scattered by the noisy progress down the narrow street of a clumsy, scarlet-hooded vehicle on four wheels, drawn by a pair of powerful white bullocks. It was a wonderful conveyance, gold-braided, tasselled, lacquered, and the trappings of the animals were gay, and sown with bells. It drew up beneath the balcony on which, a moment ago, the woman had leaned and laughed. Now she had re-entered the lighted room behind her, and the venetian doors were closed.

"That is the *rath** of Babu Chandra Das," remarked a bystander in a loud voice, for the crowd had collected again. "To-night he goes South, and the woman goes with him, for is he not rich? See, she comes forth."

The worm-eaten door of the house was pulled half open from within, and an old and ugly native female staggered out bearing an armful of bundles. This, being unexpected, raised a laugh among the youths.

During the little scene Coventry had stood by, feeling half-dazed, sickened with the sight and the scent of the violets, oppressed with a vague dread that burdened his body and spirit. He made an effort to turn to the syce and the pony that waited with drooping head and trailing harness; but something held him, kept him, as though his feet were weighted, till she came out—the woman he had seen on the balcony—and as she climbed into the red-hooded carriage her veil fell back, and the moonlight gleamed on her hair. It was then that full recognition struck at George Coventry's heart like the stab of a knife. The woman in the bazaar, who lived in the street of the dancers and such-like, who now drove away in the *rath* of Babu Chandra Das, was Rafella, his wife of the years that were over and dead.

His impulse was to run madly, blindly, after her, but horror paralysed his limbs, and he saw, as in an evil dream, the red hood with the swaying curtains disappear into the shadows.

Coventry felt a touch on his arm.

"What order, sahib? Protector of the poor, what order?" the syce was repeating.

"Make some arrangement," said the sahib, at last, mechanically; "I will walk home."

---

* Bullock-carriage.

And mechanically, too, he walked up the street, noticing nothing, not heeding the loitering figures that got in his way, that muttered abuse as he moved them aside, till he came to the corner where, years ago as it seemed to him now, his path had been blocked by the camel caravan. As by instinct, he turned into the principal thoroughfare, passing in time by the house of rejoicing. It was quieter now, the crowd had dispersed, the lights in the pans had begun to burn low, and only a faint sound of singing and music came from within the building. With quick, regular tramp he continued his way through the stifling city, meeting again the odour of badly cured hides that drifted across from the place of the workers in leather; on through the hot, still streets that led to the squalid mud suburb outside, and thence to the broad, empty road where his steps sank soundless into the heavy dust.

He was barely conscious of physical being. All the time, as he walked automatically through the bazaars, mid the heat and the smells, his thoughts had been chained to the past. Trixie might not have existed— her puzzling absence, his quest, his doubts and his apprehensions had gone from his mind. He was living once more in those far-away days that had begun with such happiness, only to end in such failure and pain; they had seemed to him over and dead, as leaves torn out of his volume of life and destroyed, and now a result had arisen, alive and awful and tragic—the woman in the bazaar! Was it a dire pre-warning, those words that had haunted his dreams and his mind in the jungle, that had harassed him in the train, followed him up to the door of his house?

Memory tortured his soul, sparing him nothing. Again he found himself riding along in a country lane on a summer morning in England; he saw the vicarage garden, the tangle of blossoming shrubs, the ragged riot of flowers, and visioned a slender figure in blue crossing the unkempt lawn, with hair glinting gold in the sunshine. A clear young voice was trilling a verse of an old, familiar hymn:

> *"Other refuge have I none;*
> *Hangs my helpless soul on Thee;*
> *Leave, ah! leave me not alone,*
> *Still support and comfort me."*

He went through it all in hopeless, despairing surrender—the simple wedding in the village church, the period of placid happiness, and then the doubt, the jealousy, the torment of suspicion, culminating

ALICE PERRIN

in that dreadful night—the night of the ball. It returned to him now with cruel distinctness; he could see Rafella running to the door, her white arms lifted as she struggled with the bolt; he heard her fleeing from him through the compound. . .

"Other refuge have I none——" But she herself had chosen to seek other refuge, knowing full well what she did! Should he have tried to prevent her, to understand her distress, her condition of mind? She was frightened, indignant, and helpless, whatever her fault; and he had allowed her to go, had made no effort to save her, because he was blinded with fury, was jealous and hard, and perhaps unjust. . . What was the story of all those years? He sickened to think. What had she suffered, endured, to bring her to this—poor little fair Rafella, with her gentle ways and her narrow knowledge of life?

"Still support and comfort me——" He remembered her protest— how shocked she had been at his personal rendering of the words, how he had said in the rain that morning—the morning on which he had told her he loved her—that he meant to protect and support her as long as he lived. How had he kept his vow?

"Leave, ah! leave me not alone——" Yes, he had left her alone, had been harsh and unyielding, without patience, without pity for the "helpless soul"; he had put her away, condemned her unheard, abandoned her to her fate. . .

He walked on, his head bent, his heart racked with a sharp and terrible remorse; it was his fault, his alone, that she had fallen to this hideous degradation; and now there was nothing he could do. It was irredeemable, beyond his power to cancel or to atone.

As he turned into the compound his consciousness came back, as it were, to the present. The bungalow stood dark and silent, just as he had left it. Trixie was not there; he knew it, though he went inside and called her. Alarm again assailed him for her safety, and he paced the drive in nervous agitation, fearing she was ill, that an accident had happened. Never had she seemed so dear, so precious to him; that he could have mistrusted her at all now caused him shamed contrition, and all his grudging of her gaieties and freedom struck him at this moment in the light of selfishness and petty tyranny. The recognition, wakened by the bitter lesson of to-night, of how in time he might have strained her love and trust beyond endurance, filled him with acute dismay and consternation.

If he only could know that Trixie was well, had met with no harm. For the twentieth time he went down the drive to the gate, and stood surveying the road that stretched white between the shadows of the trees to the right and to the left. Away in the distance jackals were howling, and over the plain in front of the house there floated the regular beat of a tom-tom. The immediate silence around him, the moonlight, the heat, and the faint, far sounds, seemed charged with a nameless despondence that weighed on his soul. He felt indescribably wretched and weary. Fever was creeping again through his veins, and his limbs and his head ached sorely. He turned at last and went back to the house, intending to order a horse to be saddled that he might set out again to search for Trixie; but as he reached the veranda the sound of wheels and the trotting of a horse came faintly to his ears. He stood still and listened.

Chapter 13

The Outcome

Guy Greaves and Trixie Coventry drove through the gateless entrance to the colonel's compound, that was sentinelled by whitewashed pillars built of mud, and drew up sharply at the foot of the veranda steps. Standing at the top of the steps they perceived a tall figure, familiar even in the ghostly light of a dying noon. At first Trixie suspected that her imagination must have deceived her; the next moment she realised that in truth it was her husband. Why had George returned so much sooner than he had intended? How long had he been waiting here for her to come back? She gave a little involuntary cry of consternation, and called to him tremulously:

"George, is that you? You are back? When did you get back?"

There was something unusual about the manner in which he descended the steps without giving an answer. She thought he was shaking with anger. When he spoke his voice sounded odd, almost as though he were drunk.

"I got back," he said slowly, picking his words with care, "not so very—not such a long time ago. The servants said you were out—you had gone out to dinner—with Mrs.—with Mrs. Roy——."

Trixie stood up in the dog-cart. George had put out his hand to help her down; his face looked haggard and drawn, his eyes were sunk deep in his head. As she alighted he steadied her trembling form, and glanced up at the young man sitting, dumb with surprise and alarm, in the trap.

"Thank you for bringing my wife home, Greaves," said Coventry, with laborious courtesy. "See you to-morrow, perhaps. Good-night."

"Good-night, sir," came a respectful and relieved response; and without looking back Guy Greaves drove rapidly out of the compound.

Husband and wife stood alone on the steps of their veranda. For a space neither of them uttered a word. Trixie's heart beat painfully; she waited for George to speak, almost choking with apprehension. Was he dreadfully angry? What was he going to say? Wild visions of futile explanations and excuses, followed by disgrace, despair, even perhaps divorce, crowded her mind and rendered her weak and helpless. She yearned to throw herself into his arms, to feel his lips on hers, to weep out her love and her contrition on his breast. He stood there beside her, handsome, tall, to her adorable. Had she lost him through her foolishness, her lack of will? She dared not speak; a little sob was all the sound she made. Then suddenly she became conscious that George was swaying slightly as he stood. He began to say something, still in that odd, unnatural voice, but now the words were without coherence.

"George, are you ill?" she asked in quick concern, a concern that ousted all other distress for the moment.

He put up his hand to his head which was burning and throbbing with fever, and tried to control his wandering senses. He wanted to speak and tell Trixie not to be frightened. He was vaguely aware that she feared his reproaches, his anger; on her arrival her face and her voice had betrayed it, and she had trembled, poor child, as he helped her out of the dog-cart. He wanted to ask her easily, gently, where she had been, what had happened, with natural intonation, to make her believe that whatever she told him, of course he should quite understand. Instead he knew he was saying something entirely different, and he found himself powerless to prevent it. Trixie looked dim, indistinct, and her voice sounded far away, at the other end of the compound.

She was asking, alarmed and bewildered: "What do you mean? Dearest, what is the matter?"

He groped for her hand as though he were blind. "I was trying to tell you," he said thickly, "that I—that I"—he made a desperate endeavour to hold to his purpose, but failed—"I wanted to tell you about the woman in the bazaar." Then he reeled; and his wife, exerting all her strength, half supported, half dragged him to a chair.

A FORTNIGHT WENT BY, AND at sunset one evening Trixie Coventry came out of the bungalow to stroll with lagging feet about the garden. She looked white and weary, yet relief was in her eyes for suspense was over, George was gaining strength. His illness had been sharp, a vicious form of fever contracted in the jungle and encouraged by the journey, as well as by all that had followed on the night of his return. For days and nights after his collapse in the veranda he had either raved and tossed, or lain exhausted and inert scarcely conscious of existence. Fortunately a good nurse had been available, and, as is usual in India, people had been immeasurably kind and helpful. Yet the strain had been severe for Trixie, the watching, the anxiety, the long hot nights, the dread until the doctor could, with truth, assure her that her husband would not die;

and underneath it all lay the harrowing uncertainty of what George had been about to say to her when delirium had intervened. Nothing in his wanderings had given her the smallest clue. As frequently happens when sickness causes derangement, the subject nearest his mind had seemingly fled. He babbled of trifles, of things that had never occurred, and complained with fractious persistence that a tortoise-shell cat with no eyes would sit on his bed.

Now that was all over, and the terrible weakness that followed had been fought with uninterrupted success, till now he was able to sit propped up in a chair, though looking perhaps, as he said himself, "like a famine-relief-wallah—nothing but eyes and bones." Yet, so far, he had uttered no word to set Trixie's mind at rest on the subject that haunted her thoughts and leavened her joy in his convalescence. His manner, at least, was the same as of old towards her, lover-like, and in addition so grateful for all her care; but she was conscious that sometimes when she was moving about the room, his eyes were fixed on her with an expression she could not define to herself, a mixture of patient interrogation, and—was it doubt? Often during the last two days, now that he was able to talk without subsequent loss of strength, she had resolved to make herself speak, and explain; but always something had stopped her, either her courage had failed, or the nurse had come in, or he had said something commonplace just at the moment which seemed to render that moment unsuitable for a confession.

Then this morning, just as she thought she had nerved herself up to the point, he had suddenly asked her to write to Guy Greaves.

"Tell him I want to see him," he said; "tell him to try and come over this afternoon."

She had glanced at him nervously, swiftly; his voice told her nothing, he might have been bidding her ask any one of his friends in the station to pay him a visit. Also his head was bent, he was patting one of the dogs, so his face was not visible. Therefore she wrote the note without question or comment, and wondered how Guy would feel when he got it!

She avoided Guy when he arrived in the evening; and now, while he sat with George, she was strolling about in the garden, uneasy and restless. The lawn looked scorched and hard, despite generous watering that now seemed hardly worth the labour and expense for the water only dried, hissing, as it reached the earth, raising a little steamy vapour that dispersed, leaving everything as hot and dry and arid as before. The evening had brought neither coolness nor sweet scents, and it seemed difficult to determine whether the heat came from the dull yellow sky, or from the cracked earth beneath. Birds stupefied with the close atmosphere held open their dry beaks as though gasping for breath, shrubs and trees drooped thirstily.

Trixie noted it all with a sense of personal detachment from her surroundings. The heat was intensely trying, but this being her first hot weather she did not suffer so much as if she had lived longer in the country. She was suffering more from the shock and the strain of George's illness than from the actual heat, and also she awaited the appearance of Guy Greaves from the house with an agitation that was painful. Not that she feared any longer such exaggerated possibilities as had tortured her imagination on the night of her river adventure with Guy, when her mental perspective had been blurred by remorse and vexation. She could almost have laughed, recalling the fear of disgrace and divorce that had assailed her so wildly; what harassed her now was the thought that her husband might never believe in or trust her again, that his confidence in her might never be fully restored. And with this apprehension was mingled a sense of resentment that George should have sent for Guy to ask him about that tiresome night on the river before she had told him herself. Perhaps he imagined she did not intend to tell him at all, or perhaps he had planned to elicit the truth from Guy, so that by no possibility could she deceive him! Well, if that were his motive then nothing should make her explain; she would answer no questions, and offer no single excuse. George could content himself with whatever he had been able to get out of Guy; if he liked he might even suspect her of waylaying Guy and concocting the plausible story of accidental delay! The old defiant temper arose within her, obliterating for the moment all her late repentance and her chastened mood.

She had worked herself into a state of unbearable tension by the time she caught sight of Guy Greaves in the veranda. He came down the steps looking absurdly young; there was something rather sheepish and ashamed in his demeanour, like a schoolboy fresh from reproof concerning some senseless prank. Trixie waited for him, feeling angry and contemptuous. She would have liked to bid him tell her nothing of what had passed between himself and George, but human nature could not be resisted.

"Well?" she said with ungracious reluctance, dispensing with formal greeting.

"How do you mean? How did I think he was looking? It has knocked him about a bit certainly. I got quite a shock at first when I saw him, but he declares he feels splendid, and he talked no end. I hope it hasn't tired him awfully."

"You know perfectly well what I mean. What did he say to you about that night?" She hated herself for asking the question, and hated Guy also for making her ask it.

"He said nothing at all about it."

"What?" cried Trixie, amazed and incredulous.

"Fact," said Guy, and nodded his head, regarding her gravely. "I tell you I was in a blue funk when I got your note, and you told me nothing as to how the land lay. You might at least have let me know that everything was all serene. He never mentioned the subject, and, of course, I wasn't going to begin."

Trixie's natural gumption failed her for once. In the moment of sudden reaction, following on her suspense and emotion, the fact escaped her that Guy was assuming she had put matters right—had explained the whole thing to the colonel's complete satisfaction.

"But"—the words came from her lips involuntarily—"I felt certain he had sent for you to ask you about it!"

"Good Lord! then you hadn't told him?" They gazed at each other in mutual discomfiture. "And he said he wished I'd take you for a drive because you'd been bottled up looking after him all this time and it would do you good. By gad," he concluded, "he's a stunner, and to think that we ever imagined——"

"How dare you say 'we'!" cried Trixie unfairly. "Didn't I tell you it showed how little you knew him?"

"Well, you needn't rub it in," he protested; "and if it comes to that——"

Trixie flushed, and her eyes filled with tears. "Yes, I know," she said helplessly, "it's no use pretending——"

For a few moments they stood silent, so motionless that a grey squirrel whisked across the grass between them and shot up the nearest tree elated with his own daring. Daylight was fading rapidly, in a short time it would be dark; the sultry heat of the evening seemed to grow more oppressive. Insects were humming around them, and bats had begun to swoop low over the lawn.

Guy Greaves broke the pause. "I suppose," he said indiscreetly, "it's too late now for a drive."

"*A drive!*" echoed Trixie, with scorn. "I'm going in now to tell George what I think of myself—and him."

"And what about me?" asked the boy, a forlorn sort of humour pervading his tone.

"You don't count," Trixie told him with heartless candour. "Nobody in the world counts with me except George."

She moved towards the bungalow, a slender white form in the dusk. Guy watched her go up the steps; then he gave a little wistful sigh and summoned his trap.

George was still in his chair when Trixie entered the room. At the far end she could see his head and shoulders silhouetted against the opposite open door. The lamps had not yet been lighted, and a powerful electric fan kept the air in motion, creating a semblance of coolness. Was he asleep? She stole softly round the back of the chair and knelt by his side.

"Trixie?" His arm went round her; she pressed her face against his.

"Shall I tell you now," she asked, "or are you tired?"

"Tell away," he encouraged her cheerfully, in prompt understanding.

There was a pause; then he found she was crying.

"Darling!" he urged with concern. "Whatever you tell me I shall believe—of course."

"Oh, George, I love you, I love you; but I was frightened. I didn't know what you might think. Really I hadn't—hadn't done anything *awfully* wrong."

"I know, I know," he soothed with tenderness, and waited, stroking her hair until she grew calmer. "Well? How did it happen? Don't tell me unless you like; it won't make any difference."

"Oh, but I want to explain," she began once more. "You know, that evening, the night you came back, it was so hot and so lonely, it seemed as if the time would never go by—and I let myself be persuaded into dining with that rowdy little Roy woman. We all went on the river afterwards because there was such a moon; and somehow, *not* on purpose, I went in a boat alone with Guy Greaves." She paused again, reluctant to "give away Guy," yet anxious to make no concealment. The pause and a little unconscious movement signified mental unease; Coventry guessed what had followed and came to her aid.

"And then, I dare say," he suggested good-humouredly, "young Guy made an ass of himself, and you were obliged to squash him?"

"Oh, George, how did you know?"

"Never mind. Well, let us skip that part and proceed. What happened next?"

"Then we got stuck on the sandbank. I thought we should be there all night, perhaps till after you had got home next day." She shivered, recalling her anguish of mind.

Slowly the tale was unfolded, till she came to the walk through the dust in the road, and then she omitted, without hesitation, her quarrel with Guy regarding her husband, and the qualms it had caused her of which she was sorely ashamed; so she unwittingly spared him a measure of extra pain.

When she had finished he kissed her lips. Words were not needed between them now. She laid her head on his shoulder with a sigh of supreme content, feeling ineffably happy. . . The room was almost in darkness; the only sound within it was the whirring of the fan.

Coventry drew his wife into his arms; he knew she was wholly his. Love and tenderness flooded his heart, that yet ached with a load that could never be lightened. For even as he held her, sweet and silent, to his breast, his conscience cried the bitter truth—that always must he owe the saving of her love, and of her trust, to the woman in the bazaar.

A Note About the Author

Alice Perrin (1867–1934) was a British novelist born in colonial India. As the daughter of a Major General, she received a quality education in England. After she married, Perrin moved her family back to India, where she raised her son. She rose to fame for her portrayal of British life in colonial India and maintained a publishing schedule of releasing a novel every two to three years. At the end of her career, Perrin had completed seventeen novels, many of which were bestsellers.

A Note from the Publisher

Spanning many genres, from non-fiction essays to literature classics to children's books and lyric poetry, Mint Edition books showcase the master works of our time in a modern new package. The text is freshly typeset, is clean and easy to read, and features a new note about the author in each volume. Many books also include exclusive new introductory material. Every book boasts a striking new cover, which makes it as appropriate for collecting as it is for gift giving. Mint Edition books are only printed when a reader orders them, so natural resources are not wasted. We're proud that our books are never manufactured in excess and exist only in the exact quantity they need to be read and enjoyed.

Discover more of your favorite classics with Bookfinity™.

- Track your reading with custom book lists.
- Get great book recommendations for your personalized Reader Type.
- Add reviews for your favorite books.
- AND MUCH MORE!

Visit **bookfinity.com** and take the fun Reader Type quiz to get started.

Enjoy our classic and modern companion pairings!